P9-DDB-523

## ALSO BY PETER CAMERON

# CORAL GLYNN

# CORAL GLYNN

## PETER CAMERON

FARRAR, STRAUS AND GIROUX

NEW YORK

Farrar, Straus and Giroux
18 West 18th Street, New York 10011

Distributed in Canada by D&M Publishers, Inc.
Printed in the United States of America
First edition, 2012

Library of Congress Cataloging-in-Publication Data
Cameron, Peter, 1959–
    Coral Glynn / Peter Cameron — 1st ed.
      p.    cm.
    ISBN 978-0-374-29901-9 (alk. paper)
    1. England—Fiction    I. Title.

PS3553.A4344C67 2012
813'.54—dc23
                                    2011034926

Designed by Jonathan D. Lippincott

www.fsgbooks.com

1    3    5    7    9    10    8    6    4    2

The author wishes to express his gratitude to Jonathan Galassi,
Katherine MacEwen, Irene Skolnick, the MacDowell Colony,
and the Corporation of Yaddo.

*For Florent*

She had resolved that she would not content herself with a lifeless life, such as those few who knew anything of her evidently expected from her. She would go into the world, and see if she could find any of those pleasantnesses of which she had read in books.

—Anthony Trollope, *Miss Mackenzie*

# PART ONE

That spring—the spring of 1950—had been particularly wet.

An area at the bottom of the garden at Hart House flooded, creating a shallow pool through which the crocuses gamely raised their little flounced heads, like cold shivering children in a swimming class. The blond gravel on the garden paths had turned green, each pebble wrapped in a moist transparent blanket of slime, and one could not sit on either of the two cement benches that flanked the river gate without first unhinging the snails and slugs adhered to them.

The excessive moistness of the garden was of no concern to anyone at Hart House except for the new nurse, who had arrived on Thursday, and had attempted, on the two afternoons that were somewhat mild, to sit outside for a moment, away from the sickness and strain in the house. But she found the garden inhospitable, and so had resolved to stay indoors.

She was the nurse, officially at least, only to the old lady, Mrs Hart, who was dying of cancer. Her son, Major Hart, who had been wounded in the war—he seemed to be missing a leg or at least part of one, and moved his entire body with an odd marionette stiffness—did not, officially at least, require a nurse.

Coral Glynn was the third nurse to arrive in as many months; it was unclear what, exactly, had driven her predecessors away, although there was much conjecture on the subject in the town. First it was supposed that the Major was perhaps a Lothario, and had made disreputable advances, although he had never acted that way

before—in fact, he had always seemed to hold himself above romance of any kind. Then, when the second nurse, who had been
quite old, fled as fleetly, it had been assumed that Mrs Hart was
impossibly difficult, since dying people often are, and Edith Hart,
even when in the bloom of health, had tried one's patience. The new
nurse—the third—was young again, and was expected to be seen
escaping, either from unwanted seduction or abuse, on any given day.

There was one other person in the house besides Coral and
Mrs and Major Hart: an elderly woman named Mrs Prence, who
acted as cook and housekeeper. Before the war there had been a
real cook and a maid, but now all the burdens of the household fell
upon Mrs Prence, who bore them with a grudging dutifulness.

Hart House was several miles outside of Harrington, in Leicestershire. It stood upon a slight rise in the water meadows beside the
river Tarle, near the edge of the Sap Green Forest. There were no
other houses within sight, for the meadows often flooded, and the
air was damp and considered bad.

The night of her first day in the house, Coral came downstairs
after putting Mrs Hart to bed to find her son standing in the front
hall. The old woman, though very ill, insisted upon continuing the
monotonous daily motions of rising and dressing; her bed was made
and she was moved to a chaise longue where she napped and fret-
ted, wrapped in a blanket, until she had had her supper, after which
she was undressed and washed and put back into bed. This was a
complicated endeavour, as it was a high four-poster, onto which she
needed to be hoisted, as she could no longer climb the few wooden
steps that ordinarily provided access. She refused to sleep in any
other bed: she had been born in this bed, she claimed (although in
fact she had not), and would die in it, too. Or die getting into it, more
likely, Coral thought. So she was unusually exhausted when she descended the stairs—exhausted from the combination of travelling,
arriving and settling in, meeting her new patient, hoisting her into

the ridiculous bed—and was not happy to see Major Hart waiting at the foot of the stairs, leaning over his cane. She paused at the landing and looked down at him. It appeared as though he was attempting to strike a rakish pose, but the utilitarian purpose of his cane could not be disguised.

"How is Mother?" he asked.

How am I to know? Coral thought. It is too exhausting, what people expect. Of course your mother was not well. I would not be here if she were. And since I have only arrived today there is nothing to which I may compare her health. And why did he say Mother? Why not *my mother*?

"Your mother is weak," she said. "And fretful. But stable, I think. I have given her an injection. She should sleep through the night."

"Is she in great pain?"

"No," said Coral. "The injection will alleviate any pain."

"Ah," he said, as if her answer had been clever. He was looking down at his hands. One clasped the knob of his stick and the other clasped its mate.

A clock chimed somewhere—the house was large and full of chiming or softly bonging clocks—and Coral was suddenly aware of the wind outside, the damp. The house was so far from anything. She shivered.

Major Hart looked up at her as if he had heard her. She stood very still, not wanting to move. She was so tired. She reached out and laid her hand upon the banister. She looked up at the distant coffered ceiling. She thought of how tired she was, and of the little room on the attic floor that had been shown to her, the little room that was now hers, how its narrow bed had not been made, just the bare mattress on the crude iron bedstead, elaborately mapped with ancient stains, the linens stacked at the foot. And why should I expect anything different? she thought. Who in the world should have made the bed? I should be happy the bed is there, the little room there; so many people do not have little rooms, and beds . . .

"I thought perhaps . . ." Major Hart began, but faltered.

"Yes?" she said, and she could hear in her voice her exhaustion, her dismissal of him, so she said it again, "Yes?" in a softer way.

"I thought perhaps you might like some brandy—or some tea—before the fire. But perhaps you're too tired."

"No," she said. "Thank you. Some brandy—a little brandy— would be lovely."

"It's just that I'm sure it's been a long day for you," he said. He took some awkward shuffling steps backwards, opening a space at the bottom of the stairs, and she descended.

"Yes," she said. She touched her hair and followed him into the dark library, the drapes all drawn, a downcast lamp on the desk and a fire glowing quietly in the grate. He turned his chair around so that it was facing the one that had been drawn up close to the fire, positioned there, she sensed, for herself. He poured some brandy into a glass and held it out to her, and for a moment she didn't take it, just let it glow there, ambered in the firelight between them. It seemed such a gift.

"Thank you," she said. "Very kind."

He said nothing, and she could not make out his expression in the gloom. He had a soft, handsome face and although his hands shook, his face had an utter, almost eerie calm.

"Aren't you going to have any?" she asked.

He did not answer but poured another glass. He held it towards her, but the fire had shifted, and the liquid remained dark. "Welcome to Hart House," he said.

Coral touched her little glass neatly to his, and then retracted it, and sipped. It was lovely, burning; it collected her around herself, gave her a centre. She thought that she might weep for a moment— the brandy had that power, too—but she knew enough not to.

They sat in the chairs drawn near to the fire.

"I hope you will be happy here," he said. "I hope my mother will not be too much of a burden to you."

"Oh, no," she said. "She is not a burden at all. No patient is."

"Yes, I suppose, if you look at it that way," he said.

She wasn't sure how to reply, so she said nothing.

"Where do you come from?" he asked.

"Huddlesford," she said.

"Oh, Huddlesford," he said.

"The spring is late here," she said.

"Yes," he said. "It is always late here."

"You're from here?" she asked.

"Yes," he said. "I grew up in this house." He looked up at the ceiling and then around the dark room, as if some trace of his long habitation of the house might be apparent. "Do you have family in Huddlesford?"

"No," she said. "My parents are dead."

"And there is no one else?"

"I had a brother," she said. "But he was killed in the war."

"Where was he?" asked the Major.

"El Alamein," she said.

"Ah," he said, "the desert. The first or second battle?"

"The first," she said. "July sixteenth."

"I'm sorry you lost him."

Coral made no reply. The Major looked down into his brandy and sipped it. Then he looked over at Coral.

"Did you nurse in the war?" he asked.

"No," she said. "I was too young."

"Of course," he said. "Of course you were. I'm sorry."

"I would have liked to," she said.

"For how long, then, have you been nursing?"

"Two years," said Coral.

"And you always do this kind?"

"What do you mean?"

"Do you always nurse patients in their homes?"

"Yes," said Coral. "Private nursing. It's hard to get jobs in hospitals—there are so many nurses from the war."

"Yes," he said, "I'd imagine so. Do you like it—private nursing? You are not lonely for home?"

"No," she said. "This suits me."

"You go from place to place? Job to job?"

"Yes," she said.

"And where is home?"

"I have no home," she said.

"Really? No home at all?"

"No," she said, and there was something final about this admission, something defeating, as if the lack of a home precluded any further conversation. They attended their brandies. Soon her little glass was empty. She stood. "Thank you for the drink," she said. "Good night."

"Good night," he said.

She put her glass on the mantel and left the room. She climbed the stairs, leaving him below, alone—submerged, it almost seemed— in the dark.


One fairish afternoon when Mrs Hart was sleeping, Coral went down into the kitchen. Mrs Prence was sitting at the table reading a magazine, but she looked up and watched Coral descend the stairs.

"Good afternoon, Mrs Prence," Coral said.

"Good afternoon," said Mrs Prence. She returned her attention to the magazine.

"I was thinking to go out for a little walk," said Coral. "I wondered if you might suggest a place to go."

"A walk?" asked Mrs Prence, with some suspicion.

"A little walk," she said. "Not far. Just to get some fresh air."

Mrs Prence made an odd noise that made clear her opinion of fresh air.

"There is nowhere to walk?" asked Coral.

"There is the whole world for walking," Mrs Prence declared.

"I thought perhaps there was somewhere scenic to walk."

Mrs Prence made the noise again.

"Well," said Coral, "I suppose if I set out, I shall find something."

"There is a wood across the river," admitted Mrs Prence.

Coral, whose pride was injured, did not ask for details.

"If you go out the gate at the bottom of the garden and turn right, and walk along the river, you'll come to a footbridge. Cross it, and you'll be in the Sap Green Forest. There is a path. People walk there."

"Thank you," said Coral.


The sky was low; there was either a heavy mist or a light rain—it was hard to discern. But Coral would not be deterred by something as inconsequential as weather. The little pool in the garden had spread and there was barely room to walk around it. Her shoes squelched in the puddling earth. The gate was swollen shut and had to be forced. She wondered how long it had been since it had been opened. The river ran fast and full and lapped avidly at the sides of the little footbridge, and it was almost dark in the woods, and unnaturally quiet. Or naturally quiet. She passed a large copse of holly trees, larger than any she had seen, their metallic leaves glinting cruelly in the dark forest. For a moment she thought she heard someone crying. She paused and realised it was just the weird sawing of the holly leaves, chafing in the wind.


On the few afternoons when it wasn't raining and Mrs Hart slept soundly, Coral walked in the Sap Green Forest. She explored the different pathways through the woods, each of which emerged, surprisingly, into a different world: a churchyard, an abandoned aerodrome, the overgrown garden of an old house, the water meadows. The woods were not very large, she realised, but there was nevertheless a feeling of isolation in the centre of them.

One day as she emerged from the woods onto the path that led to Hart House she saw a solitary figure standing on the footbridge. It was a gloomy afternoon, slurring towards darkness, and there was something foreboding about the tall dark figure standing perfectly still on the bridge, like a sentry. Her instinct was to turn around and hasten back into the woods, and wait for the figure to disappear before she returned to the house, but she realised that she had been seen; the figure raised a hand in greeting, and kept his arm raised, as if he were hailing a cab. It was the Major.

Coral looked behind her into the wood, as if there might be a similar figure summoning her from the opposite direction, or as if there might be a figure behind her whom the Major hailed. But there was nothing, no one, just the dark craw of the forest, so she was forced to move forwards and join the Major on the footbridge.

"Hello," he said as she approached. "Fancy meeting you here."

"Yes," she said.

"Been for a walk in the woods?" he asked.

"Yes," she said again, as if that were the only word she knew.

"It's a shame about the weather," he said. "Such a wet spring. Still, it must be nice for you to get out of the house."

She was about to say yes again but stopped herself.

He looked at her then—they had both been gazing at the still-swollen water rushing beneath them—and though she felt his gaze, she did not return it, but continued to study the water, as if trying to look through it for something lost at the bottom. After a moment he looked away at the woods she had vacated and said, "I used to know the woods very well as a boy. Walk in them, and play in them. They were much larger then, and wilder. Well, not wild, not wild at all, of course, but they seemed wild to me. A child's perspective." He paused, as if she might comment on his memory, but she did not, so he continued. "It's difficult for me now, to walk in the woods, the ground is so uneven. I do all right with my stick as long as it's flat. Pathetic, really." He tapped his cane against the railing on the footbridge.

"What happened?" Coral asked. She looked at his cane, but they both knew she was looking at his legs. He wore green tweed pants and brown leather laced boots. The boots were perfectly polished and the leather looked rich and supple; they were a lovely chestnut colour.

"My injury?" he said.

"Yes," said Coral. "I wondered, but perhaps it is something about which you do not care to speak."

"I suppose your being a nurse—"

"Yes?" said Coral.

"I suppose, your being a nurse, these things interest you."

"Well, no," said Coral. "I only wondered."

"Most girls. Well, girls are funny about injuries, aren't they? Damages. But I suppose nurses aren't."

"I only wondered," Coral repeated, once again apparently betraying the dearth of her vocabulary.

"I damaged my right leg and the left was badly burnt. I wear a brace."

"You seem to do very well with it," Coral said.

"As I said, I can manage the straight and narrow, which I suppose is all a man like me is entitled to. Yet I miss the woods. I had a fort in the woods, when I was young, where I played at soldiering. I wonder what's become of it."

"I could help you perhaps, if you'd like," said Coral.

"Help me with what?" asked the Major.

"Help you to walk in the woods."

"I'm sorry, but that's impossible. I can't endure being led about like an invalid."

"Of course," said Coral. "I'm sorry."

"Oh, it's I who am sorry, I assure you."

Coral said nothing. A cat appeared from beneath the footbridge and sat on the bank, cleaning its paws.

"That's Pippin," said the Major. "Mother's cat. He ran away when she became ill and makes himself scarce. Pippin!" he called, but the cat took no notice. "Animals are odd, aren't they? They cope so differently from humans."

"Yes," said Coral.

"It's getting dark," said the Major. "I did not mean to interrupt your walk. You must value your time away from Mother. Like Pippin."

"Oh, no—" began Coral, but the Major turned and walked back across the bridge, towards the house. Coral waited for him to disappear behind the garden gate before she followed. While she waited, the darkness completed itself.

That evening, when Coral was returning her dinner tray to Mrs Prence in the kitchen, the Major emerged from the library.

"Oh—hello," he said, as if he were surprised to find her coming down the stairs, when it could have been no one else, unless his mother had miraculously recovered.

"Good evening, Major Hart," Coral said.

"Yes," he said. "Good evening, Miss Glynn. I wanted only to say to you—to tell you—that I am sorry for what I said to you this afternoon, and for the way I spoke."

"You needn't apologise," said Coral. "I—"

"No, I must. Please allow me. You were being kind, and I was ungentlemanly. Do forgive me."

"Of course I do," said Coral.

"It is odd," he said, "that you are more at ease with disfigurement than I. It has been difficult for me to accept how I am."

"You are fine," said Coral. "Truly, you are. You are alive."

"And now I am ashamed," said the Major. "For you are correct. I have not the slightest reason to feel sorry for myself, or to wish to be other than I am."

"I only think of my brother—"

"Of course you do," said the Major, "and how insensitive of me. Now you must forgive me for that as well."

"I must return this tray to Mrs Prence," said Coral. "I do not want to keep her waiting. And I must put your mother to bed."

"Of course," said the Major. "How is Mother?"

"She is fading, I think," said Coral. "Would you like to sit with her awhile?"

The Major looked up the stairs, towards the room where his mother lay dying. "No," he said. "We were through with one another a long time ago."

Coral could think of no reply to this admission and so she shouldered open the door to the kitchen and descended with her tray. When she returned to the hallway the Major was gone and the door to the library was closed. She stood outside it for a moment, listening, but heard nothing.

Clement Hart was a solitary man, but he did have one friend, a friend of his youth, whom he loved. He had known Robin Lofting since they were boys; they had gone to grammar school together; their mothers had been friends and they often spent the summer holidays together in Tismouth, where the Loftings rented a seaside cottage. Robin still lived nearby and they met every Thursday evening for a drink or two at The Black Swan.

"How is your mother?" asked Robin.

"I don't know," said Clement. "The same, I suppose. How dreary it is to die like that. I'd much rather a bullet through my head."

"That's a cheery thought," said Robin.

"Well, I just wish people would go when their time is nigh."

"This is your mother we're speaking of."

"Yes, and you know better than anyone I've a right to feel as I do. I wish I had a jolly, happy mother like yours."

"Oh, it wasn't all lemonade and iced cakes with Rosalie."

"Yes, but at least she liked children. Or other people, for that matter. I don't think my mother ever met a person she liked. Including my father, of course. What a wretched woman. It's all I can do to stop myself rushing upstairs and holding a pillow against her face."

"Have you got a new nurse?"

"Yes," said Clement.

"Ancient or nubile?"

"I rather like this one. She's a nice girl."

"Nubile?"

"You're such an ass, Robin. As if you ever cared for nubility."

"Nobility, perhaps. But we are men drinking in a pub, so one must say certain things, mustn't one? For appearances' sake, if nothing else."

"Oh, God. I care nothing for appearances. I'd like to go away somewhere and live a hermit's life."

"People once had hermitages, I think. To be picturesque. They'd build false ruins and follies on their grounds. But I don't think that happens much anymore. But you could be a hermit in the Sap Green Forest. Dolly could bring you casseroles."

"How is Dolly?"

"Dolly never varies. That is part of her charm. Perhaps the entirety of her charm. She is a little like a dog in that way."

"Robin, you oughtn't compare your wife to a dog."

"Oh, but I mean it in the nicest possible way. I love dogs. Except for Dolly's, of course, which are thoroughly execrable creatures. They are constant in their characters, as she is in hers. I wish you would marry."

"Why?"

"Because then we would be equal. We would both have wives. The story would be complete."

"What story?"

"The story of us," said Robin.

"It is complete," said Clement. "It ended long ago."

"But not in any formal sense," said Robin. "The narrative stopped, but it did not really end. Did it?"

"I haven't the least idea what you're talking about," said Clement.

"Oh, don't make me sad," said Robin. "You know exactly what I'm talking about."

"But it is pointless to talk about it. It is forgotten."

"I don't think it is. And the fact that we are talking about not talking about it proves this."

"Shut up," said Clement. "Go and get us another drink."

Robin went up to the bar and got two more pints of ale. As he sidled back across the crowded room, he saw his friend sitting alone at their little table in the dim lamplight, staring down at his two hands, which were placed before him on the table-top. He appeared to be studying them for some obscure reason, as if he might be asked to identify them from a large assortment of severed hands at some later date. Robin stopped for a moment, struck by the beauty of Clement's sad face, and felt his love for his friend as an almost unbearable pain.

He pretended he was a waiter and placed the two glasses on the table, one before Clement and one before his empty place. "Anything else I can get you, sir?"

Clement looked up at him, and saw the love in Robin's eyes, and looked quickly away. "Sit down, you fool," he said.

Robin sat.

Clement had moved his hands to his lap but regarded his glass of ale with the same preoccupying concentration. "Perhaps I shall marry," said Clement. "Perhaps I shall marry Coral Glynn."

"Coral Glynn? Who is Coral Glynn?"

"The nurse," said Clement. "Mother's nurse."

"Your mother didn't let you marry an industrialist's daughter. She would never allow a nurse."

"My mother will be dead," said Clement. "And besides, I am no longer beholden to my mother."

"You weren't beholden then, either," said Robin. "You were a man."

"I agreed to wait until after the war. It made no sense to marry at that time. Many people felt that way."

"If you loved Jean, it did," said Robin. "She obviously thought it made plenty of sense to marry during the war. Even if she was engaged to you."

"Well, it is all in the past," said Clement.

"Everything is in the past," said Robin. "Everything we know, that is."

"Please don't become philosophical. It doesn't suit you."

Robin leant down and sipped from his too-full glass of ale, and then picked it up and drank from it. He put it down. "Are you serious?" he asked. "About marrying the nurse?"

"Of course not," said Clement. "It was only an idea."

"Perhaps it is a good idea," said Robin.

"She is a lovely girl," said Clement. "I rather like her."

"That seems like reason enough to marry her," said Robin. "It is more reason than I had."

"And it is surely my last chance," said Clement. "I will never meet another girl again, if I become a hermit."

"You may come across some Diana in the woods," said Robin. "You never know."

"Oh, yes I do," said Clement. "If Mother dies—when Mother dies—and this girl goes away, I shall become a hermit, but not in the woods. I shall become the hermit of Hart House."

"Nonsense. The two of us will go on meeting here, and I'll drag you up to London on occasion. You may become quite a gay roué, in fact. And Dolly and I will have you over, and Dolly will invite all her buck-toothed, pigeon-toed unmarried friends, and see to it that you marry one of them. She wants you to be married even more than I."

"All the more reason to marry Coral."

"How are her teeth? And her toes?"

"Perfectly normal, as far as I remember. But I have not made a study of them."

"Perhaps you should. Or, better yet, perhaps I should. I must come and meet this nurse. I know better than anyone what kind of a girl will suit you. Or bring her to us, for dinner or something."

"I can hardly do that," said Clement. "She is here to nurse my dying mother, not socialise with me. And I have barely spoken to her, in any case."

"Then how do you know you like her? I find that the way women talk, and what they talk about, matters quite a lot. Of course, Dolly only became insufferably loquacious after she said 'I do.' Two little words, tell-tale drips, before the deluge."

"You are always so cruel about Dolly, yet I know you love her. I think you are cruel about her for my sake, and there is no need for that. I am happy that you love her."

"Well, then, it is only to make you happy that I do love her. It is my way of loving you."

This admission befuddled Clement. He said nothing.

"I will come and meet Coral Glynn," said Robin, "and decide if you should marry her. I was right about Jean, remember, but you did not listen to me then. You listened to your mother."

"How can you meet her? She is always in with my mother. Or down in the kitchen with Mrs Prence, or up in her bedroom. I have to lurk about like mad to encounter her myself."

"I am cleverer than you. I have a plan: I will come to see you, and I will trip over the hearth rug and twist my ankle or something like that, and we will have to call for her to come and attend to it, as the only medical professional available."

"That plan is absurd. She will look at your ankle and see at once that you are faking. And I'm not sure I want her looking at your ankles in any case."

"Do you think I have unusually attractive ankles? Are you worried that she will take one look at my comely ankle and fall in love with me? You rather enjoyed my feet, if I remember correctly."

"Shut up," said Clement.

"It shall be my appendix, then. Something she can't look

directly at. Or I shall feel dizzy. I will come over sick in some way that cannot be proved false or be found titillating. This is how I shall meet your Coral Glynn and decide if you are to marry her. What is she like? Describe her to me."

"She is rather pretty, I think, in a plain way."

"Well, anyone can be pretty in a pretty way. Is she dark or fair?"

"She is dark, at least her hair and eyes. And rather tall, and slender. She is very quiet and has a lovely smile."

"And what about her figure?"

"I told you—she is slender."

"Has she bosoms?"

"I was under the impression that all women had a bosom."

"Yes, but they vary in size. What size are her bosoms?"

"What an extraordinary question. Why ever would you enquire about such a thing?"

"Because, as I have previously stated, we are two men talking in a pub. We must make an effort to follow protocol."

"Then the best I can tell you is that her bosom—I do not like the word—is perfectly proportionate."

"What word do you like?"

"I do not like any word. I do not like the subject."

"Most men do. The marrying kind, at any rate. You shall have to make an effort."

"I think she likes me," said Clement. "I mean in her shy, quiet way. Not in any obvious way. But when we are together, I sense . . ."

"What?"

"I don't know. Perhaps I only imagine it. There's something, though—something strange. I mean unusual. A feeling, which I think is shared."

"And what is that feeling?"

"I would not call it a happiness. A relief, perhaps. A feeling of something alive between us. A connection, I suppose."

"Love, perhaps," said Robin.

"I would not go that far," said Clement.

"Yes, I know," said Robin. "You have never gone that far."


Saturday afternoons Coral had free. The first two weeks she stayed at the house, feeling it was too soon to take leave of it, even if it was her right. The third week she did not feel well: she was exhausted, for Mrs Hart had not been sleeping and kept crying out fearfully in the night, "More! More!" wanting the morphine, the sudden gorgeous prick of it in her worn flesh, so she spent the afternoon in bed. The fourth week she knew that a precedent must be set: she must leave the house, or she would be trapped. So she did the only thing she could think of to do, which was to go to the cinema in Harrington.

Hart House was situated as far from the bus line as it could possibly be, a mile down a road of its own. Mrs Prence claimed not to know the schedule of the bus, for she thought the town was beneath her, and avoided it.

It was a chilly day—it was always a chilly day; it was hard to believe other days would come—and damp, but the sun was shining and there was a hesitation to the chill, a feeling that if the sun just tried a little harder it might, just possibly, amount to something. She was wearing a scarf about her head, a gay silk scarf splashed with giant pink peonies, which had been a Christmas gift from the mother of the children she had cared for before coming to Hart House, three children with scarlet fever, and even though the scarf had been wrapped in lilac-coloured tissue paper, she was almost certain that it had not been purchased for her—that it had been pulled from the tangle of scarves she had seen in the woman's dresser drawer, but because the woman had been kind and the children were sweet and the house had been well heated, she had not thought the gift of the second-hand scarf mean. It was its fragrance that gave it away; it still smelt faintly of the woman's perfume, and the odour reminded Coral of that woman, that warm house in Guildford, those children, the Christmas tree they decorated in the nursery, the cat who unexpectedly released a litter of eight kittens. Of course, there was more to it than that, but there is no point in remembering misery.

Coral knew that wearing the scarf out on this day, with the chill damp breeze flattening it against her head, would hasten the evanescence of the scent—that by the time she returned to the house the scarf would smell of the bus and the cinema and cigarettes and of herself. This made her feel a little sad, but like many sadnesses she knew were inevitable, she tried to hasten its occurrence, for it was unbearable for her to experience a pleasure she knew was fleeting.

As she neared the main road she saw the bus approach, and she ran and called out, but it took no notice of her and passed swiftly by. She had to wait thirty minutes for the next bus and came late into the cinema. Slowly her eyes adjusted; she could see the rapt luminous faces offered up to the glowing movie screen, and she found a seat next to a man who put his hand on her knee as soon as she sat down, as if he had been expecting her. He kept his eyes focused on the screen, as if the parts of his body were separate, his hand a small country at the outskirts of a large empire that enjoys, simply because of its distance from the capital, the sort of autonomy that is merely a result of negligence. There was something almost tender in his gesture, as if she were his wife returning from the ladies', and in the disorienting darkness Coral was for a moment confused, and thought perhaps she was his wife and the mistake was hers, but she knew by the way his hand trembled that it was perverse, so she got up and moved further along that row and sat beside a woman who had a small wheezing dog in a carpet bag on her lap.

The film, *An Odd Marriage*, was about two twin sisters who were evidently married, unwittingly, to the same man, although how this had happened Coral could not tell. One of the sisters lived in the country and the other lived in the city and the man cleverly moved back and forth between them. The country wife was domestic and rosy-cheeked and the city wife was jaded and soigné; the same actress played both sisters. When the city wife was dying in childbirth and needed a blood transfusion that only her long-lost twin sister could provide, the husband was forced to make a decision: either reveal his duplicity or allow his city wife to die. A weakling with a thin moustache and beautiful suits, he chose the latter, and brought his infant motherless daughter down to the country wife, claiming she was an orphan of the war, and the country wife raised the baby as if she were her own, but of course the husband couldn't bear the sight of the child, reminder as she was of his loathsomeness, and so he pulled her out of bed one night and tried to throw her over the cliff into the spumy crashing surf below, but the mother, waking in the night and sensing something amiss, came running out at the last moment, and struggled to wrench the child away from the father, who cruelly revealed the true identity of the little girl before plummeting (accidentally and thrillingly) onto the jagged rocks below.

The movie upset Coral, even though there was a final scene in which the country wife was seen happily marrying the handsome widowed gentleman from a neighbouring farm who had always been so kind to both her and her daughter, while waves relentlessly crashed upon the decomposing body of the evil husband, and predatory seagulls hovered above. It was not clear why the body of the loathsome husband had been left to rot rather than given a proper Christian burial.

It was dark and raining when Coral left the cinema, and there was something further upsetting about the change in weather and light, for she did not like it when night came in this unobserved way, without transition. She walked up the High Street of the town towards where the bus had left her. Despite the rain, the street was full of people hurrying about, in that happy way people do on a

Saturday evening when they think there is only pleasure ahead of them. She did not have an umbrella and the rain coursed off the fabric domes of the passing umbrellas and soaked her, and she felt outcast, defeated, so when she passed a florist's shop that was still open and brightly lit, she opened the door and stepped inside.

There was an odour of moisture in the shop, but it was different from the cold bland wetness of the street: inside the air was softer, warmer, and perfumed with the scent of the flowers that hung their necks over the rims of the tubs all around the floor. She stood inside the door, which had steamed over, as had the windows, and although she could still hear the rain and noise of the street outside, it felt far away, as if a gap had opened between her and it.

There appeared to be no one in the shop, but from somewhere in the back came the sound of a radio playing, and she stood for a moment, listening. It was an old song her brother had played often on the piano. She could picture him sitting at the piano in the parlour, his face bright in the lamplight, his fingers fiddling the keys. He had been melancholy, one of those people who always seems to be disappointed by the world, but when he played the piano something—a tight mask he always wore; a wince almost—fell away and she had liked to see his face slacken that way.

A young man emerged from the back room. For a fleeting moment she thought it was her brother, and then remembered he was dead. The young man greeted her and walked past her to the door, which he locked. And then he flipped the sign from OPEN to CLOSED. He turned back to her. "I forgot to close up," he said.

He had an odd brown shock of hair and a narrow face. He wore a pink shirt with the sleeves rolled up, a Fair Isle vest, and brown corduroy pants with very wide legs. He had a sort of kerchief tied about his neck. Despite this odd costume she still associated him, somehow, with her brother.

"Oh," she said. "I'm sorry—I thought—"

"It's all right," he said. "What would you like?"

She had meant only to step inside out of the rain, not to buy flowers—they were a luxury she could not afford—but she felt obliged now, and then she thought of her cold little attic room in the house, of how a jug of flowers on the dresser would make it almost nice, and so she said, "Some flowers. Something small." She could not say "cheap."

"Is there an occasion?"

"Oh," she said, "no—just a little bouquet—of anything, really, I can't afford much." She had never bought a bouquet of flowers and had no idea what they cost.

"Well, come back here," he said. "I've got some nice lilies I could give you cheap."

She followed him into the back room, which was brightly lit, two large tub sinks and a long worktable covered in flowers, and another table with rows of glass vases in which identical bouquets were being assembled. It was bright and cheerful and there was a heady scent of elsewhere in the air.

"Oh, it's lovely," she said. Coral had never seen so many flowers. It seemed impossible to her, this many of a thing so beautiful. She felt in some way that all the life and warmth of the cold, drab town, of her life, had collected in this room—that she was in the hot golden centre of the world.

And then she thought how soon all the flowers would be wilted, dead, all this beauty rotting on sodden trash heaps in the back alleys.

"I'm doing the flowers for the Page wedding tomorrow," the man said. "Are you going to the wedding?"

"No," she said. "I'm just in town for the day. I don't know anyone here."

"Well, Page is the mayor and his fat cow of a daughter Marjorie is being married tomorrow and half the town is invited and they want flowers on every table. I'll likely be up all night."

She didn't know what to say. There were some flowers on the floor, yellow flowers, lilies, she supposed, and she bent down and picked them up and put them on the table.

"Those are no good," he said. "They're tired."

"They look fine," she said.

"Well, they won't do for Marjorie Page," he said. "You're welcome to them if you want."

"They're beautiful," she said, but then she noticed there was a thin edge of brown on some of the petals. But they were beautiful. She held them up to her face and smelt them. It was a sweet, unlikely scent.

"Well, take them," he said. "But they won't last long."

She picked a few more of the discarded stalks off the floor and attempted to arrange them.

"Here," he said. "Give them to me."

She handed them to him and he went to the sink and cut the long stems with a penknife, wrapped wet newspaper around the amputated stalks, and then tied them together with a lilac ribbon he unfurled from a huge roll. "Here," he said, and handed them back to her.

"Thank you," she said. "They're beautiful."

"Just don't look too close," he said, and laughed.

"No," she said, "they're beautiful. Thank you."

"Where are you from?" he asked.

"I'm nursing the old woman out at Hart House," she said. "And I'd better go. I don't want to miss the bus."

"It runs late on Saturdays."

"Yes, but I've got to get back," she said. "Thank you for the flowers."

"Oh, you're welcome," he said. "They'll rot by morning."

"Well, I shall enjoy them tonight," she said. She walked back through the front room to the door and tried to open it, but it was locked. He came up behind her, touched her back, and then reached past her, turned the lock, and pushed the door open. It was still raining. "Good night," he said.

She said good night and passed through the door, which closed quickly behind her. She heard the bolt fasten and turned round to see him walking towards the back room of the shop. The lights in the front went out. She stood for a moment in the sheltered doorway, watching him in the lighted back room, moving back and forth between the two tables, carefully filling the vases with flowers.

It was raining hard when Coral got off the bus, a hard, lashing rain. The long road to Hart House was flooded and she waded through dark ankle-deep puddles. The first moment she glimpsed the house, she knew there was something wrong, for it was all lit up, throwing light out of almost every window into the darkness. The house was kept dark because Mrs Hart, like so many old ladies, couldn't bear to spend money on anything that she considered a luxury. For a moment, upon glimpsing the glowing house, Coral had the absurd idea that they had turned all the lights on for her, to help her find her way, to welcome her in from the dark, wet night.

A car was parked on the gravel drive. The front door was locked and no one answered her knocking. She walked around to the side of the house and entered through the kitchen door, and sat at the table removing her wet clothes and shoes. The kitchen was dark and the house was eerily quiet, as if all of the energy it had had gone into illuminating it, and none was left for anything else. There was a bowl on the table half-filled with a cold, congealing stew. A glass was overturned beside the bowl, and there was a puddle of what smelt like beer on the floor. Coral was disturbed by this odd still life, and for a moment she considered fleeing, running back out in the wet night and never returning. For surely something had gone wrong.

Suddenly the overhead light snapped on and Mrs Prence ran down the stairs. She stopped when she saw Coral sitting at the table.

"There you are!" she exclaimed. "Of course it would all happen when you're away. I've had to deal with everything myself!"

"What's happened?" Coral asked.

"She's dead, that's what's happened. I went to take up her tea and she was cold as a post. I told you you shouldn't have left her."

In fact Mrs Prence had said no such thing, but it was clear she was creating her own version of the day's events.

"I'm sorry," Coral said. "I came back as soon as I could. In fact, I'm back early."

"Well, not early enough," said Mrs Prence.

"I'll go up now," she said, standing up.

"You're no use now," said Mrs Prence. "Dr Caldecott's with her. And look at my supper, and the beer all over the floor. Did you do that?"

Coral didn't answer. She righted the glass.

"And what's those?" Mrs Prence asked, pointing to the flowers on the table. "What are you doing with flowers?"

"Nothing," said the Coral.

"Nothing! You're out picking flowers while Mrs Hart is gasping for her last breath! That's a pretty picture."

Coral leant down and put her wet shoes back on. She stood up and attempted to push her damp hair into place. Then she walked towards the stairway.

"It's as like you killed her," said Mrs Prence. "At least, that's how I see it. If you'd've been here you could have done something. There's no use going up there now. It's all done and over with."


Later, when Coral came downstairs to show the doctor out, Major Hart was waiting in the front hall.

"Ah, Clement," the doctor said, "my condolences. But it's a blessing really, you know—she was in such pain, and now her suffering is over."

"Yes," said Major Hart. "Thank you for coming out on such a miserable night."

"No need to thank me," said the doctor. "I'll send Mr Carmichael out tomorrow morning for the body. And you can make your plans with him. You'll want Carmichael's, I assume?"

"Yes," said Major Hart.

"Well, good night," said the doctor. He turned to Coral. "I'm sorry to have met you under such sad circumstances, but that's often the way, isn't it, in our profession?"

"Yes," Coral said. "Good night."

The doctor patted Major Hart on his shoulder. "She's in a better place now," he said.

Major Hart agreed that she was. And then the doctor opened the door and closed it quickly behind him, for it was still raining.

Coral and Major Hart waited silently for a moment. They listened to the doctor's car start and then drive away. After a moment Mrs Prence emerged from the basement. She glowered at Coral and turned to Major Hart. "Is there anything I can get you, sir? I've got some of my Finnegan's stew I can heat up for you."

"No, thank you Mary," he said. "I'm not hungry."

"I'm sorry about your mother, sir," said Mrs Prence. "She was a fine lady. I shall miss her terribly."

"Thank you," said Major Hart. "Good night."

Mrs Prence paused for a moment, as if she expected something else to happen, and then pushed through the door.

"I'm sorry I wasn't here," Coral said.

"It was your afternoon off," said Major Hart.

"Yes, I know. But I'm sorry I wasn't here."

"Well, these things always happen at the worst times, don't they? Although the doctor's right. It's better she's dead."

Because she felt it unprofessional to agree with such a statement, Coral said nothing.

Major Hart covered his face with his hands for a moment and said, "What a miserable day."

"Would you like something?" Coral asked. "A sedative, perhaps? It would help you sleep."

"I'll have a brandy, I think," said Major Hart. "Will you join me?"

"I think—I had better finish upstairs, and then I'll go to bed. I'm tired."

"Oh, please join me for a brandy. It's the one thing you can do. You must understand that I don't want to be alone."

Coral followed him into the library. He poured them both brandies and then sat beside her in front of the fire. For a moment neither of them said anything. Coral marvelled again at the warming and restorative powers of brandy. It made the world seem almost safe.

"Your own mother is dead, you said?" the Major suddenly asked.

"Yes," said Coral.

"Do you know, I never liked my mother," he said. "She was never warm or kind to me. I'm sure she did not love me, or even want me."

"I'm sorry," said Coral. She had heard this before: people speaking ill of the dead before they were even buried. It was a way of dismissing them, she supposed, a way of assimilating the loss.

"God only knows what she wanted," he continued.

"I'm sure she loved you," she said. "In her way. All mothers do."

"Oh, I don't think so," said the Major. "Did yours?"

"Yes," said Coral. "In her way. And I loved her. And my father."

"I liked my father," said Major Hart. "He was a decent man. He died when I was eleven. I had a sister, too—Charlotte. But she is dead."

"I'm very sorry," said Coral.

"Charlotte took her own life," said Major Hart.

Coral had never heard this expression and for a moment was bemused. Then she understood. "Oh!" she said. "How awful. I am sorry."

Major Hart stood up and leant against the mantel. He disturbed the coals with the poker. "I'm sorry to be so gloomy," he said.

"You've every right to be gloomy," said Coral.

"I suppose," he said. "But I still don't like it. It can so easily overtake one . . . It feels odd, though, to be finally all alone in the world."

"You have no relatives?" she asked.

"Oh, distant ones . . . none to speak of. Have you?"

"No," she said. "Well, I have an aunt, my father's sister, but I've never known her. She cheated my father out of an inheritance, or so he claimed, so we never saw her." Coral looked into the fire, which glowed brighter as a result of the Major's interference, and a memory suddenly returned to her from somewhere deep within herself: the gold necklace. Without thinking, she said, "I remember she sent me a little cross. It was very pretty and I had nothing like it; no one in my family had any jewellery. I remember how fine the chain was, as thin as could be. It seemed a miracle to me: How could anyone make something like that? I thought God perhaps had created it. But my father made me send it back to her. He said it was barbaric."

A hiss from the fire brought her back to herself. "Oh," she said, "excuse me. I didn't mean to—"

"How could a cross be barbaric?" asked the Major.

"I don't know, but it's what he said. At least, what I remember. Perhaps my aunt was Roman Catholic. It's papist, isn't it, to wear a cross?"

"As far as I know, anyone who believes may wear a cross," said the Major. "Or any one at all, for that matter. There are no laws forbidding it."

"It was 'papist' that he said, not 'barbaric.' I remember that now. My father hated the Catholic Church. I suppose only because he hated his sister, and she was Catholic."

"Were you raised in the Church?" asked the Major.

"No," she said. "Neither of my parents was religious. They were both very practical. My brother went to church sometimes, but I think it was for the music. Do you have faith?"

"No," said the Major. "I did, a bit, until the war. It's funny: war brings some men much closer to God. Others it separates. I lost my faith—what I had of it—in the war."

They were both quiet for a moment and then he walked over to the table and picked up the decanter of brandy. "A little more?" he asked.

"No, thank you," she said.

"Would you mind if I do?" he asked.

"No," she said. "Of course not. But I should be getting to bed. It's late and—" she began to push herself up, out of the low-slung club chair, but he reached out and touched her arm.

"Just sit for another minute. Please."

"Yes," she said. "Of course." She sank back into the chair, and he returned to his.

After a moment she said, "Your mother prayed, you know. Often, at night."

"Did she? I wouldn't have thought it. She was only religious in the most conventional, unspiritual way. Are you sure she was praying?"

"Yes," said Coral. "I'm sure. I heard her."

"And what did she say? What did she pray for?"

"I don't know," said Coral. "I couldn't really make it out. But I knew it was praying. She wept sometimes, too. I'm sorry. Perhaps I shouldn't tell you these things."

"No, no," said the Major. "You're right to tell me. It just surprises me."

"Were you with her when she passed?"

"No," he said. "She was alone. Mary—Mrs Prence—took up her tea and found her. I should have spent more time with her, I know, but I couldn't bear seeing her like that, and sickrooms rattle me. Did you think it odd that I never came to her? You must think me unfeeling."

"No," said Coral. "No. I understand."

"My mother blamed me somehow for my sister's death. Or not blamed, perhaps, but she thought it should have been me."

"I'm sure she did not," said Coral.

"She did," said the Major. "She told me so, quite clearly."

"People sometimes say things when they are mourning that they don't really mean," said Coral. "I'm sure she did not mean it."

The Major put down his glass and held his head in both his hands, his face downcast. After a moment he began to sob, and shook with an effort to hold it inside of himself.

Coral watched him for a moment, curiously, as if she had never seen a man cry like that, and found it somewhat distasteful.

"I'm sorry—" the Major sputtered. "Forgive me—"

Then Coral stood and moved around behind his chair and put one of her hands on each of his shoulders, as if to hold him down, as if his sobs might cause him to levitate. She said nothing. Her gesture seemed to comfort the Major. She felt his large shuddering body quieten beneath her clasp.

He reached one arm back over his shoulder and placed his hand on hers. His hand felt warm and strangely soft, and she thought, Everyone is touching me today: the man in the cinema, the boy in the flower shop, and now Major Hart. She pulled her hands away from him and stood back.

He rose quickly from the chair and turned to her. "I'm sorry," he said. "I didn't mean to— It's only that—"

"You have nothing to be sorry for," Coral said. "I shall say good night to you now. Are you sure you wouldn't like a sedative? I could give you a mild one."

"Thank you, but no," said the Major. "I shall rely upon the brandy. Thank you for sitting with me, for talking to me."

"You're welcome," she said.

"Yes," said the Major. "Good night."

Coral turned and passed from the library into the hallway. He followed her, but stopped when she began to climb the stairs. After a few steps she turned back towards him. "Good night," she said.

"Good night," he said again.

She continued up the stairs. She was aware of him watching

her, she could feel his gaze warm upon her back, but she did not
pause or turn.

What will I do? she thought as she lay in bed in her mean little
room in the attic. Where can I go now? She had thought that this
job would last for some time: Mrs Hart was dying but nowhere
near death, or so she had thought. She had always managed to move
from one job to the next without an interregnum. Would they expect
her to leave tomorrow? She would be paid, she knew, for the entire
month, but she did not think she could stay in the house that long,
eating their food; surely the hateful Mrs Prence would make that
impossible.

She remembered her aunt, whom she had not seen for years.
Forever, really, except for the strange gift of the gold necklace.
Should she seek her out? It was her father, after all, who had hated
her. Perhaps her aunt would welcome her. She knew a girl in London, from school, whom she had stayed with once a while ago for a
few weeks between situations, but she had not really liked the girl
and she knew that the girl did not like her: one evening as they sat
together in the flat the girl had asked her to breathe more quietly.
She had left the next day and been out of touch with her ever since,
except for writing her a note, thanking her for the hospitality and
apologizing for breathing loudly. It would be awkward, impossible, to go back there now.

She would telephone the agency tomorrow. Perhaps there was
another job waiting, someone who needed her and would welcome
her. Someone who wasn't terribly ill or dying. Someone convalesc-
ing from an operation or injury, perhaps, who only needed to be
kept quietly in bed. Who had a warm house. How nice that
would be!

It was raining again; she could hear it thrumming on the roof.
The ceiling sloped above her bed and she reached up in the dark

and touched it. It felt cold, and damp. She lowered her hand and
hid it beneath the bedclothes and then slipped it inside her nightgown, pressing it to her warm skin. It moved down her belly and
slid into the crevice between her legs, and she kept it there, pushed
hard against herself, as if it were containing something, or staunch-
ing a wound, until it was finally warm.

In the morning Coral went down to the kitchen and made her
own breakfast. She exchanged neither words nor looks with Mrs
Prence, who sat at the table and watched her as if she were a curiosity. Coral stood looking out the window, drinking her tea. The
rain had stopped, but it was still overcast, and the wind continued.
The bell rang and Mrs Prence glanced up at the board. She roused
herself and sighed, then trudged wearily up the stairs. After a moment she returned. She sat back at the table, faced away from
Coral, and said, "He wants a word with you. In the library."

Coral went to the sink and rinsed the cup and saucer, dried
them, and returned them to the cabinet, then went upstairs. When
she emerged into the front hall, Major Hart was standing there,
apparently waiting for her.

"Good morning," she said.

He said good morning and then: "I wonder if I could speak with
you for a moment, in the library."

"Of course," she said.

She followed him into the library. He had repositioned the
chairs so that they faced one another, not the fireplace. And moved
them closer together, it appeared. The two little glasses that had
held their brandy now stood empty on the table beside them. No—
there was a little left in the one that had been hers. She sat in the
chair and he appraised her for a moment before he sat in the other.
The proximity and arrangement of the chairs was obviously meant
to foster an intimacy; Coral tried to shift back a bit in her chair but

could not. So she folded her hands in her lap and waited for him to speak. He had bowed his head so she could not see his face and for a moment she thought he had fallen asleep, but then he raised his face to her. He was a handsome man, she realised, as if she were seeing him for the first time. His face looked different this morning: he had done something different, although she could not tell what. It was as if his features, always a bit unfocused, had been fine-tuned to a more appealing clarity; his face was more emphatically *his* face, and she wondered if the death of his mother had liberated him in some essential way.

"What will you do?" he asked her.

It seemed a strange question to her, because she had no idea what she would do: she had nowhere to go, no one to help her, just the world spreading out around the house in a bleak, inhospitable way. And it was her question, too, the question she could not answer. "Well," she said, "I'll look for a new position."

"Ah," he said, "of course."

"If I could stay for a few days, just while I arrange somewhere else to go—"

"Of course, of course," he said, almost brusquely. "It's about that that I wanted to speak with you."

"Oh," said.

"Yes," he said. He did not seem able to look at her; he studied the glasses on the table, at the golden sheen at the bottom of the one that had been hers. He spoke hurriedly: "I just wanted to let you know that if you wanted to stay here—perhaps stay on here indefinitely—that would be fine."

She was not at all sure what he meant. "To nurse you?" she asked.

"No," he said. "Not that. I am able to care for myself now. No."

"Well, if it's not to nurse you, what would I do?" And then she suddenly understood that he wanted her to work alongside Mrs Prence as a maid. And she thought, I will have to do it, at least for a time, as there is nothing else for me to do. And then she remembered the florist's shop in the town, the nice young man, and she wondered if perhaps she could get work there, and then she wondered what had become of the flowers she had brought home with her—she had left them downstairs on the table last night, but they were gone this morning, which meant that Mrs Prence had taken them, destroyed them—and then she realised Major Hart was speaking to her and she had not been listening, so she said, "Excuse me?"

"I said—perhaps it's absurd, no doubt it is—but I wondered . . . I only wondered if perhaps you would like to stay on here," he said. "As my wife," he quickly added. He had bowed his head again but he glanced up at her and then quickly ducked his head once more.

"Oh—" she said. "I'm sorry. I thought—"

"I don't mean to embarrass you. If it's absurd, just please tell me so. I only thought that since we are both alone, it might . . . you might . . . well, forgive me if I've offended you."

"No," she said. "No. Please don't think that. You haven't, not at all."

"I know I'm no good for anything," he said. "With my leg, and my condition, I'm no good for anything, certainly no good as a husband."

"No—" she said.

"I only thought that maybe—well, you don't have to answer me now, of course. No need to answer me at all. I'm sorry to put you in this ridiculous position. It's wrong of me, I know, but I thought you might leave. And so I steeled myself to speak with you before you made other plans, but of course if you'd prefer we can never mention it again."

"No," she said. "I'm just—just surprised. I didn't imagine . . ."

"What?" he asked.

"I didn't think that you—that you thought of me, or had feelings . . ."

"Of course I have feelings for you. Very warm and tender feelings. I thought I had made it quite clear last night, but that only shows how stupid I am about all of this."

"Yes," said Coral. "I mean, thank you. But we hardly know one another. And it is nice to feel warm and tender towards someone, but is it . . . a basis for marriage?"

He leant back in his chair and sighed, and covered his eyes with his hand for a moment, but quickly took it away. "Of course, you deserve more than that," he said. "You deserve . . . love. I suppose everyone does. Or perhaps not. But you do—"

"And you!" She did not want to say the word—it seemed too preposterous—so she said, "You deserve it, too."

"No, I don't. And I'm not asking for love, or even wanting it. I just want not to go all bitter and dead inside like my mother. And living here, alone, I know that I would. I can feel it already, something inside me, someone inside me, moving from room to room, shutting all the doors, shuttering the windows."

Coral was stunned by this poetic speech and could not respond.

After a moment he said, "I know this all sounds rash, and thoughtless. But I assure you it isn't. I mean, as far as I am concerned: I have thought about this. In some way, I realise now, ever since you arrived here, that night we first spoke in this room . . . but last night I thought hard about it, and it all became clear to me, what I had to do to save myself and perhaps—"

"And perhaps me?" she asked.

"No," he said. "I would not presume to think that. Or think it is in my power to do so. But I realised I could save myself, and I had to try, I must try, I must speak with you right away, before you made any plans. Before you went away. I know I shall have a better life with you than alone. I know that with all my heart, or what is left of it."

"But how?" she asked. "How do you know that? How can you

know that when you don't know me? Or is it just anyone you want to marry? Will any girl do?"

"No," he said. "You must think very little of me if you think that. Do you think that?"

"I don't know!" said Coral. "I don't know what to say, I don't really understand what's happening."

"I'm sorry," he said. "I did not mean to upset you. It was selfish of me to ask you this question, because it could not help but upset you. Of course it upset you."

"No," she said. "You mustn't be sorry. I'm not upset, I'm just muddled, all muddled, and I don't know what to think."

"Don't think now. Don't say anything more. I only ask you take a little time—or as much time as you want—to think about this later, and if it becomes unmuddled in some way, if what I am asking you, offering you—" He stopped and raised both his hands, indicating the room they sat in, and the house, the garden, the world outside of it. "Consider all of that. I know we don't know one another well. But I know you are a good person. And so am I—I assure you that I am. I don't mean that I'm good in any particular way, I don't fool myself about that, but I am not deceitful. I am kind. I'm decent. I would never hurt—knowingly hurt—you, in any way. I can assure you of that."

"But what about me?" Coral asked. "I am less sure of myself."

"Of course you are good," said Major Hart. "I have ears and eyes. I have watched you these last weeks, watched you tend my mother, watched you live alongside Mrs Prence. I have felt your calm and good—yes, good—presence throughout the house. You may not know it, but I do."

Coral did not reply.

Major Hart reached out his hand and laid it gently atop hers, so that his palm covered the back of her hand, but he exerted no pressure on it. It felt to her as light as a glove. "Say nothing now. All I ask is that you think about it, consider it. Will you do that?"

"Yes," she said. She withdrew her hand from beneath his and stood. "I will give you my answer this evening."

Coral went down to the kitchen, where her coat had been left the night before. It was still damp but she shook it and put it on, and her gloves, and tied the peony scarf about her head. Mrs Prence silently watched her, trying to discern from her actions what had transpired with Major Hart, but Coral gave nothing away. She went out the door without even looking at Mrs Prence, and walked down the sopping lawn, circumvented the pool at the bottom, which was swollen with the previous night's rain, pushed open the stuck gate, and walked towards the river. She crossed the footbridge and followed the pathway into the wood.

She tried not to think, because she did not know what to think. She hoped her answer might come to her in some way other than thinking, some surer, intuitive way, for she knew she could not decide whether or not to marry Major Hart by thinking. Major Hart! She realised she had told him she would answer him by evening because she knew she could not bear to wonder about it any longer than that.

She passed the huge copse of holly and paused for a moment, listening to the same mysterious sawing sound she had heard before. And then she heard another sound, almost human, a high-pitched wail, a shriek. It was some trapped animal, she thought, writhing in pain, and then she heard it again, the unmistakable cry of agony.

She moved aside some branches with her gloved hands and pushed herself into the thicket of bushes, and found a sort of path that led inwards. She had to bend over and hunker low to the ground to fit beneath some of the branches. The holly was thick and grabbed at her, scratching the sleeves of her coat. She heard the sound again, closer, and pushed forwards into a low-ceilinged clearing in the centre of the copse. She saw the little girl first: her hands raised above her head, the wrists tied tightly together and bound to a tree limb about a foot above her head. Her small feet just barely touched the ground, and she swung there in the queer gloom like a piece of meat hung to be dried.

And then she heard breathing and moved further into the clearing and saw the boy, who was standing a short distance from the girl, his fists full of pinecones. Many cones were scattered about the hanging girl, and her cheeks were scraped pink and raw in places, and smeared with tears. In the moment it took her to comprehend—or observe, because she did not comprehend—the scene they were all three silent, warily regarding one another as if they had all just appeared there independently of one another.

After a moment Coral said, "What are you doing? What are you doing to her?"

The girl answered. "We're playing, miss," she said.

"Playing?" Coral asked.

"We're only playing," said the boy.

"It's a game, miss," said the girl.

"But he's hurting you!" Coral said. "That isn't playing. And you shouldn't have your hands bound up like that—it will stop the circulation."

Apparently she spoke in a foreign language. "We're playing, miss," the girl said again.

"Well, you mustn't play like this," said Coral. "Untie her," she said to the boy, but he only stood and looked at her as if she would disappear as quickly and mysteriously as she had appeared. She turned back to the girl. "Do you want to play this game?" she asked.

"Yes," said the girl.

"It's Prisoner," said the boy. "We take turns."

"I don't think it is a good game for you to play," said Coral. "Why don't you play another game?"

Neither of the children answered her. There was something polite about the way they regarded her, patiently, tolerating her interruption. "I don't think it's a good game at all," she weakly amended.

"We like it," said the girl.

"Well, you must be untied, in any case. Untie her hands," she said to the boy.

He looked at her.

"You must untie her hands," she said again, "and give me the rope."

"It's my rope," he said.

"Well, then you must promise me you won't tie her up again."

The boy continued to look at her blankly, as if he had not heard or understood her.

"Fine, then," Coral said. "I shall untie her myself." She went near to the girl and tried to uncoil the rope that held her hands against the branch above her head, but it was tied very tight and she could not unloosen its knot.

"It's all right," said the girl. "We're only playing."

"You aren't playing," said Coral. "He's hurting you. Look, you have welts round your wrists."

"They go away," said the girl. "We make a mush with moss and things. It takes the red away. It's part of the game."

Coral could not think of what else to say or do. The children seemed curiously removed from her, as if they were a slightly different species. "Well, don't play too long," she said, in a tone that she tried to make final, convincing. Then she turned and moved back into the tunnel, crawled forwards a bit, and then stopped and listened. She heard nothing, only the chafing of the leaves.


When Coral returned to the house from her walk, the undertaker had arrived with his son, come for the body of Mrs Hart. Coral watched them carry the coffin down the stairs, out through the front door, and slide it carefully into the big black car. The radio was playing in the library, but the door was closed. She went upstairs to strip the bed in the sickroom, but first she opened the windows, which the old lady had never allowed: she had insisted on keeping the doors and windows shut, as if a sealed chamber could prevent death from entering, or life from leaving her.

# PART TWO

Mrs Prence had accepted the news of Coral Glynn's engagement to Major Hart with surprising, almost suspicious equanimity. They had told her the day after they had agreed to be married, and she had wished them both many happy years and disappeared down into her kitchen, but emerged a few hours later and asked if she could have a word with the Major, privately. Both the Major and Coral welcomed this interruption, for they had been sitting in the drawing room—a large cold room on the north side of the house where the furniture was arranged with the apparent goal of setting every piece as far apart from any other as was possible; where one had the sense that every object had been carefully placed decades ago and never again moved—attempting to converse with the light and cheerful tone of the newly affianced, but it did not come naturally to them, and they had been observing a strained and inexorably lengthening silence when Mrs Prence appeared with her request.

So Major Hart was pleased to stand up and say, "Of course you may, Mary," and led her into the library, leaving Coral sitting alone on the edge of her chair, perfectly still.

She was not sure how long the Major was gone, because as soon as he and Mrs Prence left her alone in the drawing room, she sank into a sort of trance, and sat in dumb stillness on her chair, one more petrified object among all the others in the room. She seemed to be fascinated by one particular object, for she stared intently at it: on the occasional table between the two French doors stood a large glass dome, sheltering a tree branch, upon which six tiny stuffed hummingbirds were affixed. Something about the stillness and permanence with which the iridescent birds clung to the branch entranced Coral. Frozen within their glass dome, their wings flared to suggest flight either imminent or recently accomplished, they were eternally poised in that second between the past and the future.

When the Major did return to the drawing room, he found it necessary to cough several times in order to rouse Coral from her reverie. She stood up quickly from her chair as if she had been caught doing something naughty and said, "Oh!"

"Didn't mean to startle you," said Major Hart.

"Oh, you didn't," said Coral, ridiculously. "I was just—thinking about something . . ."

"Of course you were," said the Major, as if that could not possibly be the truth. "Well, I have just had an interesting chat with Mrs Prence."

"Oh?"

"Why don't you sit down?" asked Major Hart. "Come sit here, beside me, on the sofa."

Coral looked at him as if he had asked her to join him in the bathtub. There seemed to her to be something unbearably intimate about sitting on the same cushion with him: it symbolised a closeness they had not yet achieved. But since she was engaged to be married to him, she could hardly refuse.

She sat on the sofa and he sat beside her, leaving a bit of a no-man's-land between them. She had never been this close to him; she could feel the warmth of his large body and realised he wore a scent, something clean and bracing, almost antiseptic but not: somewhere within it was a piney, earthy musk that reminded her of the stilled air inside the holly copse.

"Mrs Prence has very kindly alerted me to a situation that requires our immediate attention," he began. "She was sure it would have occurred to you, had you not been so excited by our engagement."

"Oh," said Coral. "What is that?"

"It is very simple, really: now that we are engaged to be married, it is—well, it isn't proper for us to live here together, under the same roof. You must understand how people talk."

"Yes," said Coral. "I do."

"Then you understand why we must live apart until we are married?"

"I was only waiting for you to suggest something," said Coral. "Of course I understand." She thought: But I don't understand anything. It was like waking up in a foreign country.

"I knew you would. I don't give a damn for what people think of me, but Mrs Prence knew that you would want to be careful with your reputation, as you are something of a stranger in our midst. So I've booked a room for you at The Black Swan and will drive you there now. Mrs Prence has kindly offered to pack your things."

Why is she packing my things? wondered Coral. Why does she want me out of the house in this sudden way? What is her plan? No, she thought: He wants me gone, he's realised I'm a dolt, regrets it all, and wants me gone, so he can plan an escape.

"I know this is all rather sudden, but we thought it best to get you safely settled in the Swan before tongues began to wag."

"But no one knows," she said, "so how could anyone possibly talk?"

"You have no idea of how quickly news—especially of this sort—travels in a small town like Harrington."

"But none of us has left the house—"

Mrs Prence entered the drawing room holding Coral's small battered suitcase. She held it out in front of her, at arm's length, as if there was something distasteful about it. "I managed to get everything in here," she said, "and if I've missed anything you can get it later."

"I'd like to go up to my room for a moment," Coral said.

"I'm sure I got everything," said Mrs Prence. "I turned out all the drawers."

"I'm sure you did, but please excuse me. I'd like to lie down for a moment."

"But I've stripped the bed—"

"It doesn't matter," said Coral. "I'm not feeling well." She turned to Major Hart, who stood rather vacantly in the centre of the room. "I'll come down in a little while," she said.

"Of course," he said. "Take all the time you need."


On the wall above the bed in her little room at The Black Swan was a painting of a bulldog wearing a fez gazing down at a frog wearing a pince-nez and a mortarboard. The dog had his head cocked to one side and the frog extended his curlicued tongue. Beneath the two creatures was the title *Best of Friends*.

Coral had expected Mrs Prence to have higgledy-piggledy packed her case and was surprised to find just the opposite: everything clean and carefully folded and packed with care. She wondered whether she had been wrong about Mrs Prence.

She stowed her meagre wardrobe in the armoire that crowded the small room, like a fat person who takes up too much space in the lift. In one of its drawers she found a shrivelled prophylactic. For a moment she mistook it for giant grub of some sort, and such was her horror of insects that she felt relief, rather than disgust, upon realizing what it was.

She remembered the father of the children with scarlet fever, the husband of the woman who had given her the second-hand peony scarf, calling it a rubber Johnny when he had slid it over his erect penis before he had done what he did to her. She closed that drawer and opened the one beneath it, which was mercifully empty.


There were two dress shops in the town and Coral went to the better one, proclaimed so even by its name: Dalrymple's Better Dresses.

Two mannequins in the window stared implacably out onto the High Street. A sign at their feet announced THE NEW LOOK.

She had never bought a better dress before and she did not know how to go about it. She entered the shop, setting a bell on the jamb to pealing, and stood just inside the door.

The beaded curtains that separated the shop from a back room were janglingly parted and a woman, in a dress similar to the ones the mannequins wore, strode forwards.

"Good morning!" she cried. "So lovely to see you! Come in, come in!"

The friendliness of this greeting upset Coral, as she was braced to be ignored or even humiliated, and did not know how to respond to this woman's aggressive good cheer. "Good morning," she managed to say.

"Come in, come in," the woman repeated. "I don't bite. Are you looking for something special?"

"Yes, I suppose," Coral said. "A dress."

"Well, you've certainly come to the right place. Day or evening?"

"What?"

"What kind of dress are you looking for? A day dress or an evening dress?"

"Oh," said Coral. "I'm not sure."

"Well, is there an occasion?"

"An occasion?"

"Yes. A party or something. A christening, or a dance. Somewhere special you'll wear the dress."

"Oh, yes. A wedding."

"A day wedding?"

"Yes," said Coral. Although they had not selected a time, she could not imagine their being married after dark.

"A church wedding?"

"Oh, no. At the magistrate's."

"Well, in that case a lovely day dress would do nicely. Is there a particular colour you like?"

"It must be black."

"Black? You're joking! You can't wear black to a wedding."

"But you see, his mother has died," Coral said. "Quite recently. He's in mourning."

"The groom, you mean?"

"Yes."

"Well, that doesn't mean you have to wear black, my dear. Unless you're family. Are you family?"

"Excuse me?"

"Are you family? Are you related to the groom?"

"Oh, no. It wouldn't be right."

"Well, it all seems very odd. Are you sure he's mourning? He oughtn't be getting married if he is."

"Oughtn't he?"

"No, he oughtn't. Unless there are mitigating factors."

"I don't think so," said Coral.

"Well, I don't think you need wear black. In fact, I think it would be in poor taste. Surely the bride won't be wearing black."

"Oh, but I am the bride," said Coral.

"You're the bride!"

"Yes," said Coral. "I am."

"I'm so sorry. I didn't understand. I beg your pardon."

Coral felt it safest to say nothing at this point.

The woman peered at her. "This isn't perhaps Mrs Hart we're speaking of?"

"Yes," said Coral.

"Ah—then you must be the girl set to marry Major Hart."

Coral did not deny this.

"I have sold Mrs Hart many a dress over the years," the woman said. "Was it Major Hart who sent you here?"

"Yes," said Coral. "He suggested here or—"

"Tiddlywinks? I don't think you'll find anything remotely suitable there. I've got a lavender silk that would look beautiful on you. Take off your coat and hat and let me get a good look at you."

Coral removed her hat and coat.

"Just throw them on the pouf, my dear," the woman said.

Coral was bewildered.

"The pouf! The tuffet!" The woman pointed to this so-called piece of furniture and watched as Coral lay her shabby coat and tired hat upon its elegant tufted surface.

"All right, now turn around. All the way round. Lovely. You have a very nice figure—a bit of a tummy, but a girdle will take care of that. And your chestnut hair is just right for the lavender. It will bring out the sheen. Add an egg to your shampoo for sheen. It comes in fawn, too, but I think the lavender is better for you. And nicer for a wedding."

Major Hart stood up abruptly when Coral entered the dining room of The Black Swan. Having not seen him for several days, she was struck again by how handsome he was; as if to make up for his imperfect body, he always dressed and groomed himself with almost excruciating attention. She could not help smiling as she made her way across the room. Everyone watched her, and she felt happy and safe, but then there was an awkward panicked moment as she approached the table when they both realised they must greet each other publicly in some physical way, but he seemed to recover his wits before she and reached out for her hand and leant forwards and kissed her cheek.

"Hello, hello," he said. "What have we got here?" He nodded at the silver box she carried.

"I bought a dress for the wedding," she said. "At Dalrymple's."

"Splendid! I hope you like it."

"Oh, I do. It's lovely."

"Good," he said. "Sit down, sit down. I'll find someone to take the box away for you." He reached out his arms and she handed him the box. "Sit down," he said again, almost tersely.

She sat down. She realised she should not have carried the box into the dining room. Now she knew why everyone had been looking at her: it was with derision, not admiration, that they had stared.

He handed the box off to a passing waiter. "Perhaps you can find a place for this in the cloakroom," he said. He sat across from her at the table. "Well, well," he said. There was a small dish of radishes on the table and he held it out to her.

"No, thank you," she said.

"I love a good radish," he said. He selected one and bit it in half. There was something almost savage in this action that took her aback for a second. "What colour is it?"

She was thinking about the radish so the question perplexed her. "The radish?" she asked. It was an odd colour—almost pink but still red.

"No, no—your dress. What colour is it?"

"Oh," she said. "It's lavender."

"Lavender?" He seemed suspicious.

"Yes," she said. "But not really—it's more a grey. A dove grey."

The waiter who had taken away the box returned and handed them both menus. "Would you like something from the bar?" he asked.

"Would you like a sherry?" Major Hart suggested.

She said that, yes, she should like a sherry.

"Dry or sweet?" the waiter asked.

"Sweet, please."

Major Hart ordered a pint of bitter.

The waiter left them, and they both studied their menus. They held them in front of their faces, like masks. Like shields. The waiter returned with their drinks, placed them on the table, and then stood, waiting. Major Hart lowered his menu. "Do you know what you'd like?"

She lowered her own and said, "I will have the plaice."

"And to begin?" asked the waiter.

"Melon," she said.

"I'm sorry," said the waiter, "but we have no melon. It isn't in season. We do have a fruit salad."

"Is it tinned?" asked Major Hart.

"I'm afraid it is," said the waiter.

"How about the prawns?" asked Major Hart.

She had never eaten a prawn and did not think this was the time to begin. "I'll have soup," she said.

"Consommé madrilène or Scotch broth?"

"Scotch broth, please."

"I'll have the prawns," said the man. "And the chop. Well done."

The waiter collected the menus and hastened away.

Major Hart drummed the table with his both his hands and looked about the dining room. After a moment he stopped his drumming and raised his beer. "To us," he said.

She lifted her glass of sherry and sipped. It was unpleasantly sweet and as thick as syrup. It was an odd colour, too: an almost orange robin red.

"Mrs Prence sends her regards," the Major said.

Coral found this difficult to believe. "Did she?"

"Yes," said Major Hart. "She did."

"When will she be leaving?"

"Who?"

"Mrs Prence."

"Leaving?"

"Yes. She won't be staying, will she, now that we're to be married?"

"Of course she will," he said. "Why would she leave?"

"I just thought—I mean, we won't need her, will we? It's only the two of us. We don't need a cook."

"Can you cook?"

"A bit," she said. "And I can learn. I'd like to. I've often cooked for myself—simple things."

"Well, of course you can cook if you'd like—Mother sometimes did—but that doesn't mean Mrs Prence will be leaving. Hart House is her home. She's lived there longer than I. Where would she go?"

The waiter returned and carefully lowered a bowl of soup at her place and a silver parfait glass of tiny foetal prawns at his.

A sheen of grease adorned her Scotch broth. She watched it wavering, recovering from its disturbing journey from kitchen to table. "I don't understand," she said.

"What don't you understand?" Major Hart asked, when the waiter had left them.

"Everything!" Coral said. "Why Mrs Prence—"

"I don't see what's so difficult to understand." He pierced one of the prawns with his fork and dandled it in the catsup. Then he lifted his fork and thrust forwards his head and swallowed it.

She said nothing. She rowed her spoon through the greasily iridescent soup.

He eliminated another prawn from the glass in the same savage manner. There was something barbaric about him, she realised. He ate as if the battle had not already been won and the food might bite back at him. He looked at her. "You haven't tasted your soup. Is it as hot as all that?"

"Yes," she said. "It is." One of the tears that were sliding down her face fell in the Scotch broth.

"Coral! You're crying," he said. "What's wrong?"

She laid her soup spoon beside the bowl and stood. "Excuse me," she said.


When she emerged from the ladies' he was in the hallway.

"I'm sorry if I upset you," he said. "I sometimes don't know how to behave about certain things. Many things. You must forgive me." He extended his arm to touch hers, but something about the way she stood there, her arms folded across her breast, prevented him from completing the action, so that his arm hung in the air between them for a moment, his fingers extended. Then he curled them into a fist and let his hand drop.

"I'm sorry," she said. "I'm just upset."

"Yes," he said. "Of course. Shall we return to our meal?"

She nodded and followed him back into the dining room. Once again everyone watched her, but their glances were covert, and she felt ashamed. Their soup and prawns had been cleared away. She was glad to see the soup gone; it was good to have the white blank tablecloth between them: a new beginning.

"Is it about Mrs Prence that you are upset?"

"Yes," she said. "She has been unkind to me. She doesn't like me."

"Mrs Prence? That's very odd. I have always known her to be a very kind woman. And I know my mother felt the same about her. Are you sure? Perhaps you mistook her meaning."

"I am sure. She has said very unkind things to me."

"Well, I will speak with her. I am sure there is some misunderstanding between you. Women often misunderstand one another, I am told."

"I don't think there is any misunderstanding between us."

"Of course you don't," said the Major. "It is not your fault. Nor hers, I am sure. That is the nature of misunderstanding, isn't it?"

She was saved from answering him by the appearance of the waiter with their food. When he had left them, Major Hart said, "Have you really got no family?"

For a moment the question confused her, as if there was a trick in it: Could you have none of something? "Yes," she said. "Well, only my aunt. The one I mentioned."

"A shame," he said. "I ask because we'll need witnesses, of course. I thought there might a relative that could stand up for you."

"No," she said.

"A friend, perhaps? You mentioned a girl in London."

"No," she said. "We've lost touch. There's no one, really."

He reached across the table and grasped her hand, squeezed it tenderly. This contact seemed to discomfit them both, so he quickly withdrew his hand and said, "How is your fish?"

"Very nice," she said. "How is your chop?"

"Adequate," he said. "Listen, about the witnesses. Seeing as how you've got no one, I wonder how you'd feel about using my friends Robert and Dorothy Lofting? They're lovely people; I was at school with Robin, and Dolly's mother and mine were close friends. They're both almost like family to me. They'll do very nicely for witnesses—that is, if you're amenable."

"Of course," she said.

"Oh, splendid. Splendid! They've invited us to dinner this evening, so you can meet them."

As a result of his injuries, Major Hart had been advised to treat his burns with skin grafts, but the notion of being literally skinned alive so soon after being almost burnt alive seemed barbaric, and he had decided he would rather live with his damaged flesh. And in a sad, curious way, he realised that he even welcomed his disfigurement, for it removed him from the arena of life he most dreaded: he felt that his damaged body disqualified him as a lover and therefore as a spouse, and he felt a great relief at the prospect of thus being excused from love and marriage and all the preliminary and subsequent complications and mortifications they involved. The Major considered himself set irrevocably apart from the world of intimate relationships, and this seemed a mercy to him, for he had never felt comfortable with other people in general and women in particular, and he knew that now no one would expect him to seek a wife. He was like the lame or weak-hearted boys at school, who were excused from games, and stood on the side-lines, cheering on the healthy lads, who bungled one another in the muddy field. But the arrival of Coral at Hart House changed him, and he felt his sense of ardour—which had, he thought, been successfully and permanently repressed—welling inside him. He had exiled love—successfully, he thought—but, like an unwanted dog abandoned miles away, it had come limping home.

Major Hart's body was nowhere near as repellent as he imagined it to be. His right leg had withered within its metal brace, but the damaged skin was limited to his left leg and chest and upper left arm, yet, he felt the effect was total, in the way that a few prominent cracks in a ceramic vase ruin it entirely. And so the prospect of revealing his body to Coral was terrifying, almost paralyzing. He would have to find a way to turn out all the lights before undressing. But he knew that even the feel of his skin was disturbing. He often touched it himself, lying in bed alone: the dead skin on his torso that had no feeling left, that was as sensitive as linoleum. And then he would touch a patch of skin that had been spared, and the silken softness of it, the electric thrill of the feeling, seemed an even worse shock.

Upstairs in her little room at The Black Swan, Coral opened the silver box, peeled the tissue away, and lifted out the dress. She laid it on the bed. It looked as if a dead person lay there. She thought of Mrs Hart atop her bed, wearing one of her better dresses, waiting for the mortician to take her away.

She took off her clothes and slipped the dress over her head. It had a zipper and many hooks up the back, which she could not reach herself. It seemed very cruel to design a dress that the wearer could not don independently. Who would help her on the day of the wedding? She wondered if she could do up the dress and then wriggle herself into it from beneath. She took it off and tried this but could not fit it down around her bust and shoulders. For a moment she felt trapped within the dress. In her panic to free herself she ripped a seam.

Once again the bell jangled when she opened the door and a voice from behind the beaded curtain called out a greeting. Coral stood inside the door, clutching the silver box to her chest.

"Someone's just come in," she heard the voice say. "I'll ring you back."

And then the woman appeared through the beaded curtain. "Oh, hallo," she said. "It's you. Is everything all right?"

"I'm afraid not," said Coral.

"Oh, goodness. What's wrong?"

"The dress—"

"But it looked lovely on you! It fit perfectly."

"Yes, I know," said Coral. "But it isn't right."

"What's wrong with it?"

"I want a dress I can put on myself. I can't with this one." She held out the silver box.

"Don't be silly," said the woman. "It's a lovely dress."

"I know," said Coral. "But I can't put it on."

"Of course you can. You just need to be done up. Surely you can find someone to do you up."

"I can't," said Coral.

"You said you were getting married. You don't get married alone!"

"It wouldn't be right for him to do it," said Coral.

"Well, there will be others about, surely. Your mother, perhaps."

"My mother is dead."

"Well, a friend, then. Your maid of honour. Or matron."

"Do you have a dress I can put on myself?" Coral asked.

"Certainly not! All my dresses are fitted. But this is ridiculous. I have never heard of such a thing. I'll come do it up for you, if it comes to that."

"I couldn't ask you that. I just want a dress I can put on my-self."

"And I tell you I haven't got such a dress. Besides, part of being a bride is being fawned over. Surely there's someone—"

"I would like to return this dress," said Coral.

The woman strode forwards and practically grabbed the box out of her hands. "Very well," she said. She put the box down on the pouf and opened it. She pulled the dress out of the defiled tissue paper and held it up before her. "In all my years I have never known anything so ridiculous. This dress is absolutely perfect for you. Look—it's been torn! You've torn it yourself." She thrust the dress forwards, exposing the ripped seam. "You can't return a torn dress!"

"It tore itself," said Coral, "when I was trying to put it on."

"I beg your pardon, but my dresses don't tear themselves! You've torn the seam through some fault of your own and you're trying to return it under some ridiculous pretext." The woman dropped the dress back in to the box, pulled the tissue round it, smashed the top back on, and held the box out to her. "I'll not be party to such tom-foolery."

"I don't want it," said Coral.

"Well, I've told you, you can't return a dress that you've torn. Surely you understand that."

Coral said nothing.

"Do you? Do you understand that?"

"Yes," said Coral. "But I don't want this dress. I don't need this dress. I am not getting married."

"Oh," said the woman. "Well, that is another thing entirely. Your plans have changed?"

"Yes," said Coral. "My plans have changed."

"I am sorry to hear it. But you know, I would be more than happy to mend the seam for you, and you can wear the dress on another occasion. Surely you can. It is that kind of dress."

"You are very kind," said Coral. "Thank you. But I don't want the dress." She turned and left the shop, left the woman holding the silver box, and stepped out onto the High Street.

On the way back to The Black Swan Coral passed the florist's and saw the young man who had given her the flowers through the flower-filled window. She stood outside the shop window for a moment, and he looked up and saw her, and smiled at her, and waved. She pushed open the door and entered the shop.

"Hello," the young man said.

Coral said hello. She stood just inside the door, once again amazed at all the flowers, the perplexing abundance of them. "How do you know," she asked, "what to order?"

"Beg pardon?"

"How do you know what flowers people will want? They don't last long, do they—flowers?"

"Well, there are tricks," he said. "And people tend to want the same things, over and over, or certain things at certain times of year. But mostly they simply want what they see. Flowers are nice in that way. Would you like something?"

"Oh, no," she said. "I'm looking for a job. Do you need someone here?"

"I thought you were a nurse," said the young man.

"I am," said Coral. "I was. But I don't want to nurse any longer. I can't . . . I'd like to do something else. Something like this—" and she indicated the flowers around them.

"Do you have any experience with flowers?"

"No," she said. "But I'm good with my hands." She held them out, as if the fact that she had hands was proof of this. "And I could learn . . ."

"Well, I don't know," he said. "We don't really need anyone else at present."

"I could clean," she said. "Or anything."

"I'll speak with Mrs Lippincott. She's the one who owns

the shop. What's wrong?" he asked, when he saw that she was crying.

"Oh," said Coral. "I've done something awful. I've been so foolish, so stupid . . ."

"What have you done?" he asked. He came around from behind the counter, removing the handkerchief that crested out of his jacket pocket, and handed it to her. "Here you are," he said.

She felt the silkiness of it and saw its beauty, and although it featured a pattern of dogs chasing foxes, it did not seem a proper handkerchief for a man. "Oh, it's so lovely," she said. "I couldn't. I've got my own." She handed it back to him and opened her purse and found her own drab hankie, and dabbed at her nose and eyes.

"Is it about marrying Major Hart?" he asked. "Is that why you're upset?"

"Where did you hear that?" she asked.

"Oh, it's the talk of the town. People tend to gossip at a flower shop."

"But I'm not getting married," said Coral. "I was—perhaps I was—but I'm not. It's all a muddle, an awful, stupid muddle, and I don't know what to do."

"Why aren't you getting married?"

"Do you think I should marry him?" Coral asked.

The florist laughed. "How could I know? I couldn't possibly know. You're engaged to him, aren't you?"

"Yes," said Coral. "Do you know him?"

"Major Hart? No. He's quite a bit older than you, isn't he?"

"Yes," said Coral. "I suppose he is."

"And he's a rather solitary chap, by all accounts."

Coral agreed.

"But I suppose you've fallen in love with him, and there's no telling about that."

"What do you mean?" asked Coral.

"Well, it often seems quite odd to me: who loves who. Or doesn't. One sees the most unlikely couples."

"Do you think we make an unlikely couple—the Major and I?" asked Coral.

"I couldn't say, really. And wouldn't if I could. And what does it matter? It only matters what you think."

"But he's a good man, as far as you know? He seems very kind to me."

"I have never heard a bad word about him. He seems to be a perfect gentleman, so why have you changed your mind? Has he done something wrong?"

"Oh, no," said Coral. "It's nothing like that. It's so silly, so stupid, as I told you. It's all on account of the dress."

"I'm afraid I don't follow you. What dress?"

"I bought a dress to be married in, and I was stupid, and tore it, and brought it back to the shop and said I didn't need it because I wasn't to be married after all. I do things like that all the time, I don't think things through, I'm like that with everything, and everything becomes a muddle."

"Well, this seems rather a silly muddle, and one that is easily fixed."

"How?" she asked. "I can't possibly go back to the shop. I'd die of shame. You've no idea of the scene I made."

"Was this at Dalrymple's? Mrs Henderson?"

"Yes," said Coral.

"She is really very nice and I am sure you are not the first woman to have hysterics in her shop. I'm sure she will make everything right with the dress. You must go back at once."

"Are you sure? She seemed very cross with me."

"Yes, I am sure. Shopkeepers are never cross for long. She will greet you with open arms."

"You've been so kind to me. I am Coral Glynn," she said, and held out her hand.

The young man shook it. "I am John," he said. "John Shields. I am very happy to meet you, Coral."

The door to the shop opened and a man in a business suit entered. He wanted a dozen yellow roses for his wife's birthday. They had no yellow roses. Only red and cream. He took cream.

Coral watched the entire transaction. She liked John and did not want to go away.

"My brother's name was John," she told him, although this was not true. But she associated her brother with him, and her brother's name had been James, which seemed close enough.

"Was?" asked John.

"He died in the war," said Coral. "In '42. I miss him still."

"I lost one of my brothers, too, but I can't say I miss him. He was rather a brute."

"I'm sorry," she said.

This talk of dead brothers had changed the tone of their conversation, and neither of them seemed to know what to say.

Finally, John said, "Go see Mrs Henderson and set things right with your dress. And you must come to me for your bouquet. You will have flowers, won't you?"

"I don't know," said Coral. "I hadn't thought of it."

"Well, you will. I shall see to it. Unless, of course, you do change your mind."


The sky was still gently lit and the sidewalks were crowded with people hastening home for the evening when Coral left the flower shop. She paused at the window of the jeweller's next door, and leant her forehead against the glass and peered in at the glittering golden wealth.

She had not meant to steal the sapphire ring.

The woman—the mother of the children with scarlet fever, the wife of the man with the rubber Johnny—had taken the ring off and left it on the rim of the bathtub in the nursery when she bathed the children one evening. Coral had found it and meant to return it the next morning, but the woman had not missed it, and so she thought she would keep it until its disappearance was noted and a search was announced and then she could triumphantly find it, and the woman would be beholden to her, for she wanted this older woman's approval and love. But instead the woman searched Coral's things and found the ring wrapped in gauze in her syringe kit.

Curiously—or perhaps not—it was the man who saved her. He told his wife it wasn't worth ruining anyone's life over a sapphire ring, that all's well that ends well. But she shouldn't be working in people's homes, said the wife, if she's a common thief. She must be stopped. The man agreed and said that he would alert the agency.

Later that night, the last night Coral spent in that house, the husband came to her bedroom and gave her the sapphire ring and told her to keep it. At first she would not, but he insisted that she must take it with her: his wife no longer wanted it and she could always sell it one day if she needed money. And he told her he would not contact her agency. She hated that he was being kind to her after what he had done, for it interfered with her loathing of him.

She had hidden the ring behind the mirror that hung on the wall in her little bedroom in the attic of Hart House. She would have to remember to retrieve it once she returned to the house. Perhaps she would send it back to the woman—anonymously, of course, for she felt sure the husband had lied when he said his wife no longer wanted the ring. Why would she not want it?

She turned away from the jeweller's window and saw the headline, spikily chalked onto the slate propped up against the newsagent's across the street:

**GIRL FOUND HANGED IN SAP GREEN FOREST**
**MURDERER AT LARGE**

Because of a recent motoring accident involving a badger, Major Hart no longer drove at night, and so it was by taxi that Coral and he arrived at Eustacia Villa, which was the name given to the house where Robert and Dorothy Lofting resided. Eustacia Villa was a large rectangular house of only two stories, its façade composed of unadorned brick painted a chalky white with turquoise trim. Its walled forecourt was square; gravel surrounded a circular low mound of barren earth that was ringed by a miniature chain fence. One assumed flowers adorned it at some other season. A stone plinth marked the centre of this mound; on either side of the door, which was painted to match the turquoise trim, stood two large concrete urns, which, like the garden, were empty.

The Loftings stood in the lighted open doorway and watched their guests get out of the taxi. Major Hart, because of his stick, needed help from the driver. Coral stood awkwardly beside the car trying to look as if she were involved somehow with the Major's extraction. It wasn't until he was standing beside her that anyone spoke, as if it were a scene in a play that could not begin until they had all assumed their designated marks.

"Hallo's!" and "Good evening's!" were suddenly flung across the gravel, and the Loftings left their mark in the doorway and strode forwards to greet their guests.

"Robin! Dolly!"

"Clement!"

"You're looking splendid!"

"And you must be Coral. So lovely to meet you!"

"Please, call me Dolly."

"And Robin."

"Come in, come in, it's chilly out, isn't it?"

Dolly took the Major by his arm and led him towards the house.

"I saw you admiring my obelisk." Robin touched Coral's shoulder and turned her towards the aborted garden. Coral watched the taxi pass through the open gates and disappear. She felt stranded. She was not sure what she was supposed to have been admiring, but she managed to murmur, "It's lovely."

"I had it brought back from Egypt. It's fifth century B.C., used for ritual human sacrifices. Poor blokes were lashed to it and buggered to death."

"Really?" was all she could find to say.

"Course not," said Robin, laughing. "For decorative purposes only, I assure you."

"Of course," Coral said, oddly relieved.

The interior of Eustacia Villa was an odd warren of many little rooms, all of them crowded with furniture, objets d'art, ferns in cauldrons, and assorted bric-a-brac. Many of the rooms had mirrors on several walls, which lent them a dizzying fun-house effect. And they all seemed to be on slightly different levels as well. Dolly and a trio of Pekingese, who had been introduced in the entry hall as Yin, Yang, and Mabel, led them through several of these rooms, all of which appeared to be some variation of sitting room, although what differentiated one from the next, except for steps and arched doorways, was a mystery. Dolly stopped abruptly in one room that claustrophobically contained two sofas and a grand piano. The sofas faced one another, and into the little space between, a low goldpainted rattan table was jammed, and on this table was a tray of canapés that looked as they might have been waiting there for a very long time. A drinks cart was pushed up against the piano. The room was apparently deep within the interior of the house, for it had no windows, only a door at either of two ends and mirrors above both sofas.

Dolly and the dogs claimed one of the sofas. The Major indicated the facing sofa to Coral and then sat down beside her. Robin stood beside the drinks cart and rubbed his hands together.

"What would you like, Coral?" Dolly said. "Robin can mix you a cocktail if you fancy one. He's quite good at it."

"Oh," said Coral. "Nothing for me, thank you."

"A Nothing? That must be a new one," said Robin. "Never heard of it before." He turned to his wife. "What was that one we all liked so much with the crème de menthe, darling?"

"A Grasshopper!"

"That's right. You're sure to like it, Coral. You'll have one, darling, won't you?"

"Course I will," said Dolly. "I'll have two!"

"And you, old man? Nothing ventured, nothing gained."

"Just a whiskey, please," said the Major.

"Oh, don't be such a chappy chap, Clement! Make us all Grasshoppers, darling!" said Dolly.

Robin busied himself at the little drinks cart. Dolly fed each of the dogs one of the canapés and then held the tray out towards her guests. "I'm practically positive it's anchovy paste," she said, "but the label's come off the tube." Coral and the Major both took a canapé. The Major chucked his into his mouth and appeared to swallow it whole. Coral held hers delicately between her thumb and forefinger. She tried to find a place to set it down, but the table beside her was crowded with an odd community of porcelain figurines ranging from Nubian princes to Tyrolean goatherds, so she placed it on the opened palm of her other hand and held it on her lap. Perhaps she could feed it to one of the dogs when no one was looking.

Robin handed the drinks around and lifted his in the air. "To the happy couple," he said, "Coral and Clement."

"Coral and Clement!" echoed Dolly. "Oh, it's scrumptious, darling—like melted ice cream!"

Robin pushed the dogs off the sofa and sat beside his wife. He helped himself to a canapé and offered the tray across the table. The Major took one and disposed of it as abruptly as he had his first. Coral indicated the canapé in her palm by way of refusal.

Dolly took another sip of her drink and snuggled back into the sofa. She wore a little pale-green moustache. "Now you must tell us all about yourself, Coral. You must tell us everything."

But Coral could not think of a single thing to say. "It's very kind of you to ask us to dinner," she finally managed.

"Well, I am sure we will be the dearest of friends," said Dolly, "so you must tell us all about yourself."

"I can't think of what to say," said Coral. "There isn't much to tell." She turned to the Major, as if he might know the story of her life better than she, but he was staring with fixated horror at his Grasshopper.

"Nonsense!" said Dolly. "I'm sure there's oodles and oodles! How long have you been nursing? And what's your middle name and what's your favourite colour and where are you from?"

"Two years," said Coral, electing to answer only the first question.

"And where you're from?"

"Coral is from the South," said the Major, as if it were important to keep her place of origin obscure.

"Oh," said Robin, "whereabouts?"

"Huddlesford," said Coral.

"Huddlesford! That's hardly the South!" shouted Dolly.

"It's south of here," the Major declared.

But Dorothy was nonplussed. "And your family? Are they all in Huddlesford?"

"My parents were born in Huddlesford," said Coral. "But they are dead."

"Both of them!" exclaimed Dolly. "I'm so sorry. I've still got my mother. And sister, too, for that matter."

"Coral had a brother as well," explained the Major. "But he was killed in the war."

"So you've no family at all?" Dolly appeared to find this possibility thrilling.

"An aunt," said Coral. "But I haven't seen her in years."

"Well, we shall be your family now." Dolly leant across the low table and reached with both her hands to grasp Coral's, but as Coral had not yet succeeded in feeding the canapé to one of the dogs, and still held it covertly in her left hand, she could only half return the affectionate gesture.

At the same time that Coral and Clement were visiting the Loftings, Mrs Prence was entertaining a visitor of her own. The bell at Hart House had rung not long after the taxi had collected Major Hart for his dinner engagement. Visitors at Hart House were rare, and so it was with both trepidation and curiosity that Mrs Prence climbed the stairs and answered the door. A man in a mackintosh and a Bavarian hat stood on the terrace, looking up at the jackdaws having their final panicked flight across the darkening sky. He turned towards the door after a second and said, "Ah—I am Inspector Hoke. I believe you must be Mary Prence. Or are you perhaps Miss Coral Glynn?"

"I am Mrs Prence," said Mrs Prence, who had long ago abandoned her Christian name.

"Good evening, Mrs Prence. I know that visitors at this time of day are a terrible inconvenience, but I wonder if I might have a word with Major Hart?"

"He is not at home at the moment," said Mrs Prence.

"Really? I thought I would be sure to find him here. Where is he?"

"He is out," said Mrs Prence.

"I see," said Inspector Hoke. "Well, in that case, I wonder if Miss Glynn is available?"

"The nurse—Miss Glynn—is no longer here. Are you the police?"

"Yes," said Inspector Hoke, "in fact I am. Or a representative thereof. I wonder, Mrs Prence, if I might talk with you for just a moment."

"Talk about what?"

"A little girl was killed in the Sap Green Forest recently, not at all far from here. Have you heard anything about it?"

"Only what's been in the newspaper," said Mrs Prence. "It's a horrible thing."

"It is. Just as you say: a horrible thing. And since Hart House is so near to the woods, it would help me very much to talk to you, just for a moment or two. May I come in?"

Mrs Prence hesitated. The jackdaws had quit the sky and it was almost dark. It was dark inside the house, too: she had hurried upstairs from the kitchen when she heard the bell and had opened the door without turning on any of the lamps.

"Pardon me, but have you got a badge or something? You could be anyone, couldn't you?"

"Of course, of course," said the Inspector. "How very wise of you to be so cautious. I should have shown it to you immediately. Here is my identification." He pulled a wallet from a pocket inside his coat and opened it to reveal his identification. "I have aged a bit since this photograph was taken, but I believe a likeness remains."

He chuckled, but Mrs Prence did not seem amused. By way of reply, she stepped back and opened the door wider. The Inspector entered the dark house and said, "Where were you when the lights went out?"

"Pardon?" Mrs Prence closed the door.

"I was only attempting to be humorous. The dusk comes so suddenly, doesn't it? How I long for our lingering summer evenings. They are one of the few benefits of inhabiting a northern clime."

"I couldn't say," said Mrs Prence, having lost the train of Inspector Hoke's thoughts.

"Is there someplace we might sit for a moment? I should just like to ask you a few very simple questions."

Mrs Prence could not imagine entertaining the Inspector in either the drawing room or the library, so she suggested he follow her down into the kitchen, where she invited him to have a seat at the table.

"My mother always said that the kitchen was the heart of the home," said the Inspector. "Would you agree, Mrs Prence?"

"I couldn't say," said Mrs Prence, since the phrase was ready.

"Well, it is a very cosy sanctuary you have here," said Inspector Hoke.

"Would you like some tea?" Mrs Prence asked.

"Some tea might be very nice indeed, if it is not too much trouble."

"It is no trouble at all," said Mrs Prence, and lit the flame beneath the kettle.

"Very cosy indeed," said the Inspector.

Mrs Prence opened a cabinet and dropped two iced buns thunkingly upon a plate. Then she waited for the kettle to boil and filled the teapot, and when this little repast was prepared, she carried it to the table upon a tray. "Have a bun," she said, "if you'd like. Currant." She sat and filled a cup with tea and slid it across the table. Then she filled another for herself.

"Is my hunger so apparent?"

Mrs Prence was about to resort to her now standard line but stopped herself and said, "I think a bun is always nice."

"A truer word was never spoken." If the Inspector believed this, he did not act according to his principles, for he ignored the buns. He spooned sugar into his tea and then dribbled it with milk. "Now, about this horrible business in the forest. I wonder, Mrs Prence, if you have seen anyone in the area in recent weeks?"

"I stay out of the forest," said Mrs Prence. "There's nothing in there that interests me."

"I see," said Inspector Hoke. "What about around the house, or on the road? Any strangers lurking about?"

"Not that I've seen," said Mrs Prence. "Except for Miss Glynn, of course. The nurse."

"But she is not a stranger. You have seen no one else? The little girl herself, perhaps?"

"I've seen nothing," said Mrs Prence. "I'm too busy in the house to be gazing out the windows. There was a stray dog hanging about a while ago, but I didn't feed it, so it's gone. It's always a mistake to feed wild creatures—it upsets them." She nodded her head at the plate of buns that sat on the table between them. "If you think they're nasty store-bought buns, they're not. I baked them myself."

"Did you?"

"Yes. I don't believe in buying what you can make yourself. People have gotten too good for themselves."

"I'm sure there is something in what you say," said Inspector Hoke.

Mrs Prence moved the plate with the buns closer to him and kept her hand on it, making it clear she would not release it until he had taken one of the buns. He selected the smaller one and tried to place it upon his saucer, but it was too large to fit. He brought it to his mouth and took a bite, which took him a moment to process successfully. "Delicious," he said when he had finally swallowed and was able to fit the now reduced bun upon the saucer.

"Miss Glynn walks in the woods," said Mrs Prence. "She's very keen on it."

"Is she?" asked the Inspector. "Perhaps she has seen something, then. I'll have to have a word with her."

"She's staying at the Swan," said Mrs Prence. "They're getting married, you know."

"Yes," said the Inspector, "I had heard something about that."

"It's all rather odd, if you ask me," said Mrs Prence.

"Odd? In what way?"

"She's odd. There's something not right about her, if you ask me. And why are they getting married? I'd like to know. Major Hart's never been interested in that kind of business. I suppose it's because he's lost his mother and feels alone. Thinks he needs some-one to take care of him. But he's in for a nasty surprise, I've no doubt."

"Oh, really? What sort of surprise?"

"That girl is as likely to take care of him as she is to skin a rabbit. She'll take care of his money, perhaps, but not him."

"It seems that you have a low opinion of Miss Glynn."

"I have no opinion of her whatsoever," said Mrs Prence. "I just know what I see."

"And what have you seen?"

"It's not so much what I've seen as the feeling I've got. You only have to look at her to know she isn't to be trusted."

"Did she not take good care of Mrs Hart?"

"If you call killing your patient good care, then I suppose she did."

"What do you mean?"

"I mean what I said, although perhaps I shouldn't have said it."

"You think Miss Glynn killed Mrs Hart?"

"All I know is that she's fine in the morning and Miss Glynn disappears for an afternoon and before you can say Jack Sprat, Mrs Hart is dead."

"I was under the impression that Mrs Hart was very ill."

"Ill, yes, but dead's something else entirely! And who's to stop her from doing the same to Major Hart? Marry him first and kill him just the same as his mother, and who'll be sitting pretty then? I'll be afraid for my own life when she comes back here."

"Why? She has nothing to gain from you."

"Nothing but peace of mind. She knows I don't like her. I knew what she was up to from the start, and made things difficult. The night Mrs Hart died, she gave me a look that froze my blood. And I wonder now—now that you come asking these questions— what she was doing in the woods? Walking, she said, but in those nasty dark woods in all sorts of horrible weather? I think some- how that poor little girl must be tied in to it all. Perhaps she saw something—the little girl, I mean—or Miss Glynn told her some- thing. People talk to children so freely, and regret it. They think they're not listening, don't understand, but they are. They do. They've got minds like traps, children. Perhaps you think this is all nonsense, but you asked me what I think, so I've told you."

"On the contrary," said the Inspector. "You seem to have given this a great deal of thought, Mrs Prence, and your mind seems quite keen."

"Well, I only know what I see, which is what I said. There can be no harm in telling the truth."

"Did you ever see Miss Glynn talk to the little girl?"

"Not exactly," said Mrs Prence. "Not with my own eyes."

"Does Major Hart walk in the woods?"

"Goodness, no. He's lame, you know. He can walk all right for a bit, but not to go traipsing through the woods. Not like her. Like an explorer, she was."

"Do you plan to stay on here, Mrs Prence, when Miss Glynn returns as Mrs Hart?"

"I don't know. I really don't know. I'm thinking I might go live with my sister in Hovenden, but there's some bad feeling between us, so it might be unwise. So I shall probably stay, for as long as I am wanted. I know Major Hart wants me to, he said as much directly to me—you'll always have a home here, Mary, he said. But Miss Glynn is a different kettle of fish."

"But you have no plans to leave immediately, do you?"

"No," said Mrs Prence. "I'm debating it all, I suppose you could say. I've been here a very long time, and I always thought I'd take care of the Major after Mrs Hart died—because, as I said, he never seemed to be the marrying kind—but it appears as though I was wrong about that. Or perhaps he's wrong about it, I don't know."

"Wrong about what?"

"Marrying. She's made him think somehow he's the marrying kind. Are you married, Inspector Hoke?"

"I am not, Mrs Prence. I suppose I am not the marrying kind, either."

"Well, there's no knowing these things," said Mrs Prence.

"And you, Mrs Prence—are you married?"

"I am a widow," said Mrs Prence. "My husband died in the first war. I was married young, and widowed young."

"I'm very sad to hear it," said Inspector Hoke.

"His name was Arthur Gordon Prence. I had a child as well. She died in her infancy."

"How very sad. I'm very sorry for you."

"Her name was June," said Mrs Prence. "It is hard to remember these things. It has been a long time, but it is still hard."

"Indeed it is," said Inspector Hoke.

"You might think it would get easier, or that you'd forget, but you don't. At least, I do not." Mrs Prence reached out and felt the teapot. "Would you like more tea, Inspector? It is still warm."

"No, thank you," said the Inspector. "But I wonder if I might ask you for something else?"

"What?"

"To do something for me. What you have told me about Miss Glynn is most interesting, and I would like to know more about her. I wonder if I could trouble you to befriend her, and then she might tell you more, perhaps even confide in you."

"She will think it odd if I act friendly all of a sudden," said Mrs Prence. "She knows that I do not like her. I have made it plain."

"I don't mean anything unnatural or extraordinary," said the Inspector. "Nothing that would seem false to her. Just a bit of simple kindness, which, as she is all alone here, would mean a great deal to her. She could very well be desperate for someone to confide in. If she is, indeed, guilty of any wrongdoing."

"And then I would tell you all she told to me?"

"Of course not. Only if she tells you something that has bearing on the matter at hand. The girl in the woods."

"And there is the death of Mrs Hart as well. As I told you, I have my suspicions in that quarter as well."

"Well, of course, if she tells you anything about that—or any criminal activity, for that matter—I would be most interested to hear it. But if this makes you uncomfortable, Mrs Prence, please have no worries. I should understand."

"I am an honest woman," said Mrs Prence, "and it may be difficult for me to express affection when none is felt, but I consider it my duty to at least try and do as you say. I do not think Miss Glynn is a strong person, so it may not be difficult at all to convince her of false feelings."

"Well," said the Inspector, "I would be very grateful if you tried. As I said, nothing unnatural—we do not want to alarm her or cause her to be suspicious. But a little kindness goes a long way in situations like these, I have found. People who feel alone will jump at any chance for friendship, especially if they harbour worries." Inspector Hoke stood and picked up the remnant of his bun. "I shall take this delicious bun with me and enjoy it on my drive back into town. You have been most cooperative, Mrs Prence, and I thank you very much for your time and trouble. I shall leave my card here with you, and ask you to call me if you see or hear anything." He replaced the bun on the table and withdrew a card from his wallet and handed it to Mrs Prence. "Will you tell Major Hart that I was here and that I would like to have a word with him tomorrow?"

"Yes, of course," said Mrs Prence.

"And you said Miss Glynn is at the Swan?"

"Yes," said Mrs Prence, "but they are both visiting friends of Major Hart's this evening."

"I see. Then I believe my work for today is complete, and I shall trouble you no farther."

Mrs Prence said it had been no trouble at all and followed the Inspector up the stairs. After he left, she entered the drawing room and turned on a few lamps and then stood in the centre of the room. It was unusual for her to be alone in the house. Even with Mrs Hart bedridden and the Major something of a ghost, she was always aware of their presence, and it was rare for either of them to leave it, especially simultaneously. In these few moments alone in the house, she liked to think of it as her own. All the things in it, hers: the furniture, the rugs and drapes and paintings, the clothes hanging in the closets, the linen folded in the cupboards, the leather-bound books in the library, the china and the cutlery, the hummingbirds inside their glass dome, the marble eggs, the cloisonné boxes, the collection of ivory figurines and majolica. It seemed to her as if only the slightest barrier stood between her and the true possession of all these things—that it was only a matter of passing through some gossamer wall to find herself the true mistress of Hart House.

She stood in the room for a long time, and then went around it, touching things: the velvet drapes, the silk cushions, the polished wooden arms of the chairs. Such good care she took of it all, and for what? Then she went back downstairs into the kitchen. The tea things had been left on the table, and they stood there under the harsh overhead light, on display, revealed: the cups and saucers, the teapot, and the bitten-into rock bun the Inspector had said he would take with him but had not.

After they had finished dinner Dolly stood up and said, "I'll tell you what, Coral darling, let's let the men stay here and talk about whatever men talk about, and you and I go upstairs and pick out a dress for me to wear at your wedding."

Coral looked at the Major—perhaps it was time for them to be leaving?—but he was intent upon doing some sort of complicated violence to a cigar. So she stood up and followed Dolly out of the dining room, back through the maze of tiny sitting rooms, into the front hall, and up a rather grand staircase that turned twice before it reached the first floor.

Dolly led their way down a hallway past many closed doors. She paused outside one door and said, "I've got my own bedroom. You must have your own, too. It's the key to a happy marriage." Then she pushed open the door and entered the room. It was larger than any of the rooms downstairs but so stuffed with furniture that it seemed quite small. For a moment Coral assumed that Dolly had opened the wrong door, and they had mistakenly entered a sort of storage room, for the furniture was oddly spread about: a canopied bed was in the centre of the room with chairs and tables and wardrobes scattered around it. The only piece of furniture that made contact of any kind with a wall was a mirrored vanity table, its surface piled high with bottles and brushes and other accoutrements of beauty and health, and stacks of magazines, which, judging from their bloat, had been mostly read (and dropped) in the bathtub. The Pekes, who had joined this feminine exodus, jumped up into one of the chairs and snuffily burrowed themselves into the cushions. It was stuffy in the room and rather warm; an electric fire glowed malevolently in the grate. The wallpaper, curtains, and upholstery were all of the same deeply purple violets-gone-mad pattern.

"Isn't it cosy?" said Dolly, picking her way amongst the furniture towards the vanity. "I love my little room! Would you like a cigarette?" She indicated a little china donkey that sat on the bedside table and carried two baskets of cigarettes across his back.

Coral said, "No, thank you."

Dolly pulled a cigarette out of one of the baskets and said, "Watch this!" She pushed a button between the baskets and the donkey raised his tail and emitted a flame from beneath it. Dolly laughed and lit her cigarette with the flame. "I know it's naughty," she said, "but I think it's adorable. Robin brought it back from Gibraltar. I collect animal figurines." She selected one of the larger bottles from amongst the many on the vanity table and poured something into a smudged tumbler. "I've only got one glass, but we can share," she said. She offered first go to Coral.

"No, thank you," said Coral.

Dolly helped herself and sat in the chair unoccupied by the Pekingese. "Someone told me that the Duchess of Windsor always insists that her bed be in the centre of the room, even in hotels and things, because she finds it so much more convenient. And it is, isn't it? Everything else so close at hand. Sit down, darling, just push the little beasts off, go ahead and push them."

Coral was reluctant to push the dogs from the chair, so Dolly stood up and did it for her. One of the little dogs fell on its head and yelped. The dogs relocated themselves to the bed. "I know they're awful brats," said Dolly, "but I adore them. They're like children to me. I can't have any children, you know. I had a mistake before we were married and then a dead one after, so I had all my plumbing taken away. Fortunately I haven't a maternal bone in my body. And I know I'd've been an absolute dragonish mother, so it's all for the best. Although it's a shame for Robin, of course; he likes children so much. I expect you and Clement plan to have children. I'll be their godmother! That I could manage very well, I'm sure. Bring them presents and give them advice, that sort of thing. Now, you must tell me all about your dress. Clement said you got it at Dalrymple's."

"Yes," said Coral, "but—"

"Was Mrs Henderson in there? She's awfully common, you know, but she acts posh, as if she's just selling dresses for the fun of it. I hate people who try to be what they're not, but she does have some lovely things in there, I'll grant her that. So do tell me about your dress. What colour is it?"

"Lavender," said Coral.

"Oh! I think I know exactly the dress. Has it got bouclé sleeves?"

"I don't think so," said Coral.

"No, I think it has," said Dolly. "I tried it on the other day, but it made me look stout. But I'm sure it will look lovely on you, you have such a long waist. My problem is I'm so short-waisted. If it's the dress I think it is, I know exactly what I'll wear. I've got a lovely pinkish *peau de soie* that will look perfect with your lavender. I know it's to be a simple day wedding but I think we should wear hats. Matching hats, and the boys can wear matching waistcoats and ties, not matching to our hats, but matching to each other's. What about gloves? I think for a wedding, gauntlets would be nice, don't you? Matching, of course, it's important to have matching for the photos. My sister was my maid of honour and she insisted upon wearing green because she says everything else clashes with her skin—she suffers jaundice and is terribly pallid—so she wore this awful dark green velvet tea gown which looked black in all the photos and spoilt everything. I think she did it on purpose; she's terribly jealous of me. You see, she knew Robin before I did and he wasn't the least bit interested in her but she got it in her mind somehow that I stole him away from her. Robin's convinced she's a lesbian because she lives with an odd girl named Jill on an old farm near Chipping Manor. They breed white Alsatians. Clement's such a darling, but of course you know that. We thought he'd never marry because of his afflictions; he once told Robin he could never subject a woman to such a thing, but I'm sure he thinks your being a nurse makes all the difference. Ghastly things don't bother nurses much, do they?"

Coral seemed not to be listening. She sat in her chair gazing at the ceramic donkey on the side table.

"What is it, darling?" asked Dolly. "You look a bit ill. Do you feel all right?"

Coral returned to herself, and said, "Oh, yes—I'm fine."

"I'm sorry," said Dolly. "I know I talk too much. And drink too much, too, for that matter . . ." She looked down into the glass she still held. "I try and stop, I do, but I'm not a very strong person. And so very stupid as well."

"Oh, no," said Coral. "You mustn't think that—"

"It's because of fear," Dolly continued, as if Coral had not spoken. "It's why I talk too much and why I drink, because I'm afraid that something terrible is going to happen, something terribly terribly ghastly, and talking forestalls it. And drinking. I don't know why I'm so afraid. I wasn't always like this. Are you afraid?"

"Afraid of what?" asked Coral.

"Of life," said Dolly. "Of everything. And everyone."

"No," said Coral. "I don't think I am."

"If you have to think about it, you're not," said Dolly. "That much I can tell you. What's the most terrible thing you can imagine happening?"

"I don't know," said Coral. "The war?"

"Oh, I can think of much worse than that."

Dolly reached over to the bed and grabbed one of the little dogs from the heap and cuddled it against her breast. "Oh, you little darling," she cooed to it. "You're the littlest, most darlingest darling . . ."

Coral watched her for a moment and then said, "I was wondering . . ."

"What?" Dolly prompted.

"May I ask you something?"

"Of course," said Dolly. "You may ask me anything."

"Well, it's only because, as you know, I have no real friends or family—"

"Oh, yes you do, Coral darling! We are your friends and family now!"

"Thank you," said Coral.

"So, what is it that you want to tell me?"

"It's about something I saw," said Coral. "And I don't know what to do."

"How intriguing you are! What did you see? Tell me!"

"Have you heard about the girl, the one who was found hanged in the woods?"

"Of course," said Dolly. "Did you see her? Hanging from a tree?"

"No," said Coral. "But I think I saw her—the little girl—a week or so ago. I was walking in the woods and I heard a strange sound . . ."

"What sort of sound?"

"I don't know. I can't describe it. It was like an animal, perhaps, a trapped animal. I didn't know what it was."

"Yes, yes," said Dolly. "And?"

"So I walked into the woods, following the sound. In the midst of all this holly I found a little girl and a little boy. The little girl was tied up, tied by her hands, and the boy was throwing pinecones at her. I told them to stop it, to stop it right away, but they said they were playing. They said it was a game. The girl said it, too. I didn't know what to do, so I told them to stop it again and untied the girl, and then went away."

"And you think that's the little girl who was hanged?"

"I think it must be," said Coral. "Don't you?"

"I suppose it was," said Dolly. "But perhaps it wasn't. Lots of children play in the woods, I imagine."

"I should have told someone, but I didn't. And I don't know what to do now."

"I don't think you should do anything now. It's a thoroughly nasty business, it's gruesome, and you're well out of it. And besides, there's nothing you can do now, is there? I'd just forget all about it."

"But shouldn't I tell the police about the boy?"

"I suppose, but why get involved? I'm sure they'll find him, and if they don't, you can always send an anonymous letter later. You know, tipping them off without involving yourself. I could help you write it. We could do it with cut-out letters from the newspaper like they do in films. Or several different typewriters."

"So you think I should do nothing now?"

"I forbid it!" said Dolly. "You're about to be married, in case you've forgotten, and that's all you should be thinking about. Put it out of your mind and enjoy this happy time. Promise me you will."

"I don't know," said Coral.

"Look, you asked for my advice, and I've told you. I think I have a bit more experience of the world than you have, so you should really listen and do as I say. And I'm a friend of Clement's. Have you told him anything about this?"

"No," said Coral. "But I think I must—"

"Don't!" said Dolly. "Not a word. He hates any sort of nastiness, and since it's over and done with, you must keep it to yourself. It was right for you to tell me, and now you must do as I say. Do you promise?"

"Yes," said Coral, "if you think it best."

"I've never been surer of anything," said Dolly. "Trust me, darling. Oh, you poor dear. You look so awfully worried. Really, you mustn't let anything ruin your happy occasion. We get so little happiness in life, you know. Now I shall weep!" Dolly lurched forwards and embraced Coral. She laid her snuffling head upon Coral's shoulder.

For a moment Coral was stunned by this embrace, but almost instinctively reached her arms around Dolly and softly patted her back. After a moment Dolly lifted her head and touched her forehead to Coral's cheek.

Coral waited a moment and then removed her hands from Dolly's back and leant back into her chair. Dolly wiped at her teary eyes. "I'm sorry to be so weepy," she said. "I don't know what's come over me. It's been so long since I've had a real friend, you see. In London I had lots and lots of friends, but up here everyone keeps to themselves. I think we're a bit too grand for them. I'm so happy we shall be friends now—that's why I was weeping. But we shall, shan't we?"

"Yes," said Coral. "I suppose we will."

Do you think they will always go away together, after dinner, and leave us alone?" Robin asked Clement.

"I don't know," said Clement.

"It would be funny if they did."

"Funny? Why?"

"I don't know," said Robin. "It just seemed to me, for a moment, funny."

Clement did not answer.

"Well, well," said Robin. "I wish I had some champagne. Congratulations are in order."

"Why?"

"Why? Don't be an ass. You've found yourself a perfect wife. Or she's found you."

"Why do you say she's perfect?"

"Because she is. She's beautiful, sweet-natured, charming."

"How can you know that? She's hardly said a word."

"Just by looking at her, of course. I never listen to what women say. I'm sure it's an effect of living with Dolly, but all the same, all you have to do is look at Coral to know that she's a peach."

"A peach?"

"You are going to marry her, aren't you?"

"Yes," said Clement. "Of course I am."

"Then you might seem just a bit happy about it."

"I am. Of course I am. I just don't understand your gushing."

"Gushing! I hardly say calling your bride a peach was gushing. And even if it were, what's the matter of that? Someone ought to be happy about it."

"You don't think she is?"

"I was thinking of you."

"I've told you I'm happy."

"Then why mayn't I gush?"

"Because you know I can't bear falseness."

"But it isn't false. Why would you think it false?"

"Because I know you."

"Perhaps not as well as you think."

"Oh, Robin. What else am I to do?"

"Nothing. It is the natural thing."

"You have Dolly, you know. I don't want to be alone forever."

"I don't think marrying Coral has much to do with it."

"With what?"

"Being alone."

"Whatever do you mean?"

"Oh, nothing," said Robin. "You mustn't mind me."

"Of course I do. You are my dearest friend."

"I am your only friend. And you have just announced how little it means to you."

"How do you mean?"

"If you will be alone without Coral, my friendship can hardly mean very much to you. Or anything, for that matter."

Clement said nothing. He relit his cigar and puffed it back to life, and then observed its glowing head.

"You must forget all that, Robin. You have promised me you would."

"Then I have lied to you. Although I do not think it was a lie, because you knew it wasn't true when I said it."

"Of course I did. Why would I not?"

"Don't hurt me too much, Clement. Don't be cruel."

Clement said nothing, and once again evaluated his cigar's progress. "I'm frightened," he said.

"Frightened? Of what?"

"How can I marry her as I am, with my body? It isn't fair."

"What is wrong with your body?"

"You know: it is not a body to love someone with."

"And yet you do."

"Do what?"

"Love someone with it. I think you mean it is not a body someone can love. But I think you are wrong about that as well. At the very least, you cannot know."

"I can. I do. My body is repulsive."

"To you, perhaps. But you cannot decide for others. Does Coral know you were burnt?"

"Yes. She asked about my injuries, and I told her."

"And yet she has agreed to marry you. Is it really about that that you are worried?"

"What do you mean?"

"I think you are worried about a different aspect of your body."

"And what aspect would that be?"

"I think you know."

"I do not. I would not ask you if I did."

"I mean the physical aspect. The sexual aspect. The ability of your body—of you—to perform sexually with a woman."

"I have done it before."

"I know that. You did not keep that a secret from me."

"Do you wish that I had?"

"No," said Robin. "Of course I do not. I do not wish for any secrets between us."

"You have always been so honest and forthright, Robin. You know I am not like that. I wish that I were, but I am not."

"You are exactly as you should be. I would not love you so much if you were different."

"I feel that I can be with Coral as I am with you. It is something about her gentleness, her goodness. She reminds me of you. Perhaps that is why I love her. It is a chance I must take. If you love me, you must allow me this."

Robin said nothing, but got up from his chair and walked around the table. He stood behind Clement's chair and reached over his shoulder and took the cigar out of Clement's hand, then rubbed its embers out in the raspberry sauce on Clement's dessert plate. He lay the cigar on the plate and then embraced Clement from behind, reaching his arms around Clement's shoulders, crossing them, and grasping the two soft mounds of Clement's chest in his hands. Clement sat stiffly. Robin lay his head on Clement's left shoulder so that his lips just grazed the skin of Clement's cheek. Finally, Clement reached up one of his hands and held it against one of Robin's and Robin felt his friend's body relax within his embrace, and he held the warmth and softness of Clement in his arms until they heard Dolly and Coral approaching, and by the time the two women entered the room Robin was back in his seat and Clement was holding his bloodied cigar.

When the taxi had passed through the gates of Eustacia Villa and was travelling along the country road, Major Hart reached across the backseat and found Coral's hand in the dark. He squeezed it and then laced his fingers through hers. He looked at her, but she was staring out the window.

"Darling, you were lovely," he said. "Robin said you're the nicest girl he's met in ages. Did you like them?"

"Oh, yes," she said. "They're very nice."

"Did you have a nice chat with Dolly?"

"Yes," said Coral. "Very nice."

"Oh, good. I do hope you'll be friends. Dolly's a bit too chattery for my taste, but she's a nice enough girl. But Robin—he's the decentest chap I know. It will be nice to have them beside us when we're married, won't it, darling?"

"Very nice," Coral said, wondering at the Major's sudden proclivity for endearments. It was as if his version of their romance had sped past hers and was careering forwards, leaving her stranded in the dust at the side of the road. Perhaps it was merely that he had drunk too much. In any case, it was not unpleasant. She turned her hand over and clasped the Major's. "Could we get married sooner than next month?"

"I suppose," said the Major. "But next month is rather soon."

"I think we should do it sooner," said Coral. She thought: Dolly can do up my dress. I can get the dress back tomorrow; the woman can't have sold it with the torn seam. "Now that everything is settled—I mean the dress, and the witnesses—I don't like waiting. It makes me anxious, and staying at The Black Swan . . . it feels so unsettled."

"You want to be at home," said the Major. "Our home."

"Yes," said Coral. "So mightn't we do it sooner? As soon as we're possibly able?"

"How about Saturday next? That gives us a week to settle things."

"But what is there to settle?"

"Well, there's Dolly and Robin, for one thing. And I want to plan a proper wedding luncheon, at the Swan. And a wedding trip, perhaps."

"A luncheon—for whom?"

"Well, for us, of course. And Dolly and Robin. And Mrs

Prence. I believe it is customary to invite the magistrate. And of course anyone you would like to invite."

"Could we have flowers? A bouquet, and boutonnieres, I mean, and perhaps some on the table, at the luncheon?"

"That is precisely the kind of thing we need a day or two settle," said the Major. "We must have the absolute best flowers."

"I've met the boy at the flower shop. He was quite friendly to me. Perhaps we might invite him?"

"To do the flowers, you mean?"

"No. Well, yes. But also to the luncheon. And Mrs Henderson at the dress shop." If I invite her to the luncheon, Coral thought, she will have to be kind to me about mending the dress.

"I don't think it's customary to have tradespeople at a wedding luncheon."

"But they're not," said Coral. "I mean, perhaps they are, but they've been so kind to me, and I have no friends at all here. And you have Dolly and Robin—"

"They are your friends now," said the Major.

"Yes, but not— Oh, please let me invite them. It will make it more of a party, won't it?"

"Well, Mrs Henderson, perhaps, but I hardly think we need the boy from the flower shop."

"But why not him—if we have Mrs Henderson?"

"It's just that—the boy from the flower shop . . . It will seem very odd to everyone, I think."

"Odd? Why?"

"Coral, be reasonable. This is to be our wedding luncheon. One usually invites one's close friends and family."

"I realise that. But I have no close friends or family. Only people who have been friendly to me, like Mrs Henderson and John."

"And I said you might invite Mrs Henderson."

"But not John? It makes no sense to me."

"You may not realise these things, but there is a difference between a woman who owns a dress shop and a boy who works in a flower shop."

"And what is the difference?"

"I cannot explain it to you. It is something one either knows or doesn't."

"Is it about class? I am no better than the boy in the flower shop, if it comes to that. My father worked at that post office."

"It has nothing to do with class."

"Then what is it?"

"Can't we simply agree not to have the boy from the flower shop at our wedding luncheon?"

"I have told you, his name is John. John Shields."

"It makes no difference what his name is."

"Then what is the difference? Is it the difference between women working in dress shops and men working in flower shops?"

Clement sighed. "There is no difference. Invite John Shields, and Mrs Henderson, and whomever else you would like to have. It will make for a strange party, but if it will make you happy, I see no reason not to. Let people talk. They always do."

"Yes," said Coral. "They do."


How about a nightcap in the bar?" the Major asked as the taxi drew up in front of The Black Swan.

Coral was too tired to think of a decent way of refusing this proposal. "What about the taxi?" she said.

"Oh, Allard will wait for me, won't you, Allard? I'll make it worth your while."

"Certainly, sir," said Allard.

"I'll stand you a pint if you'd like," said the Major.

"Thank you, but no, sir. I don't drink on the job."

"Very wise of you," said the Major.

A few travelling salesmen were sitting at the bar. The tables were all empty, and the Major and Coral sat at one built into a

wood-panelled nook. "I fancy a pint of ale after that disgusting trea-
cle Robin served us. What about you, darling?"

"Just a lemonade, please," she said.

"Are you sure? You wouldn't like a glass of ale?"

"Perhaps just a glass," Coral said.

"Righty-o," said the Major.

While he was standing at the bar, Mrs Raleigh, the proprietress
of The Black Swan, entered the bar and approached their nook.
"Good evening, Miss Glynn," she said.

Coral said good evening.

"I feel it is my duty to tell you that the police were here this evening, wanting to have a word with you."

"The police!"

"Yes," said Mrs Raleigh. "They wanted to talk to you about the
girl found in the woods. You've heard about it, haven't you? A little
girl hanged by her neck and cut to pieces. Out in the Sap Green
Forest."

The Major returned and placed a tumbler of ale in front Coral
and sat down across from her, holding his pint. "Good evening,
Mrs Raleigh," he said.

"Good evening, Major Hart," said Mrs Raleigh. "I was just letting Miss Glynn know that the police have been here this evening,
wanting a word with her. And yourself as well, for that matter."

"Good heavens! The police! Whatever about?"

"About the girl found hanging in the woods. Haven't you heard,
Major?"

"I saw something in the paper."

"A little girl hanged by her neck out in the Sap Green Forest.
Quite near your house, Major, so of course Inspector Hoke would
like to speak with you all."

"Of course," said the Major.

"Wants to know if you saw anything fishy, I presume. He's already had a word with Mrs Prence."

"We would be happy to speak with the constable."

"I don't think 'happy's' the word, Major Hart, under the circumstances."

"You're absolutely right, Mrs Raleigh. It's shocking."

"Horrifying, I call it. A sweet little girl brutally murdered. What's the world coming to, I ask you?"

"Well, it's certainly not the world it was," said the Major. "We can agree on that."

"Everything's gone topsy-turvy since the war," said Mrs Raleigh. "I blame it all on Mr Hitler."

"Well, he must certainly take his fare share of the blame," said the Major.

"I'm sure he wouldn't look twice at a little girl hanged from a tree."

"I think we're upsetting Miss Glynn, Mrs Raleigh," the Major said.

"Oh, I beg your pardon, Major. I'll leave you be. The constable said he would be here first thing in the morning."

"Very well," said the Major. "Good night, Mrs Raleigh—and thank you."

"Good night, Major. Good night, Miss Glynn. I'm sorry if I upset you."

"Not at all," Coral said. "Good night."

Mrs Raleigh had a word with the barman and left the room.

"What nasty business," said the Major. "Did she upset you, darling?"

Coral found the Major's penchant for endearments more upsetting than anything Mrs Raleigh had said. "No," she said. "It's just the police . . . They upset me."

"What, don't tell me you're on the run from them!" the Major chuckled. "Well, it's just a word with us they want. Have to do their jobs, you know."

"Yes," said Coral. "I suppose they do."

•

Robin stayed downstairs and drank for a while, then went up to bed. He was surprised to see the door to Dolly's room open, and light spilt into the hallway. He paused in the doorway and looked into the room. Dolly sat upright in the bed, reading a book, the dogs deflated atop the coverlet. "Darling," she said when she saw him standing there.

"I thought you'd be asleep," he said.

"I'm reading the new Ruby Ferguson. I think I shall be up half the night. Come, sit with me a moment." She pushed one of the dogs aside and patted the spot beside on her bed.

"I'm tired," said Robin. "I'll leave you to enjoy your book."

"No, darling," said Dolly. "Come and sit. Just for a bit."

He paused for a moment and then entered the room. He sat somewhat awkwardly upon the bed, one foot on the floor and the other dangling off its side. Dolly lay the book splayed down upon her lap and reached out and touched Robin's face. "Darling," she said.

He moved his head so that his cheek fit more perfectly into her curved palm and tried to smile.

"Oh, darling," she said. "You're sad, aren't you?"

"No," said Robin. "Why would I be sad?"

"You lost him a long time ago," said Dolly, "but you feel you're losing him again."

"No," said Robin. "I'm happy for him. It's all very jolly."

"Oh, darling," said Dolly. "Lie down beside me. Just for a while." She reached over and turned out the bedside lamp and it was dark in the room, only a faint glow of light from the hallway that reached only as far as the foot of the bed. Dolly scooted over and rearranged the dogs. Robin removed his shoes and lay down atop the coverlet. Dolly reached out and put her arm around him and drew him closer, so that his head lay upon her breast. She played with his hair. For a moment neither of them said anything. Except for the wheezing breath of the dogs, there was no sound.

And then Robin said, "What did you think of her?"

"She's like a little mouse," said Dolly. "A frightened little mouse."

"Is she pretty?" asked Robin.

Dolly thought for a moment. "Yes," she said. "But in a very ordinary way."

"Clement is besotted with her, I think."

"Of course he is, darling. Poor Clement. He'd fall in love with a laughing hyena if it walked into the house."

"No," said Robin. "He loves her, I think."

"It's what I just said," said Dolly.

"But you meant not really," said Robin. "I think he does. Really."

"And it makes you sad, doesn't it?" asked Dolly.

"Perhaps," said Robin. "A little."

"I can see how you're disappointed. Poor Robin. Poor, darling Robin."

"Don't," said Robin.

"But I shall," said Dolly. "Poor, darling Robin. My poor, darling Robin. Sleep here with me tonight. Be a good boy." She placed her hand upon his forehead and stroked the hair away from his face. "Will you sleep here with me tonight?" she asked. "Please?"

"Yes," Robin said. He sat up and stood beside the bed. "I'll be right back."

He walked down the hallway into his room and changed into his pyjamas. Then he used the toilet and brushed his teeth. He shook a few drops of Penhaligon's Blenheim Bouquet into his hands, patted his cheeks, and then ran his hands through his hair. In the mirror he still looked very handsome. He smiled at himself because he had good teeth and was more handsome when he smiled.

Dolly had pushed the dogs off the bed and had moved to the far side, where she lay facing away from him. There was something impressive about the landscape her body created, something formidable and noble. She had turned the covers back for him and he climbed into bed and curled himself against her. He reached his arm around her and she clutched his hand and clasped it to her breast. They both felt his cock growing hard. In a moment, he knew, she would turn to him, weeping, for she always wept on those rare occasions when they made love.

Coral was still in bed when she heard a knock on the door. She got out of bed, put on her robe, and opened the door. A maid stood in the hallway. "Good morning, miss," she said.

Coral said good morning.

"Beg pardon for disturbing you, miss, but Mrs Raleigh says to tell you Inspector Hoke is here. He'd like to speak with you."

"Thank you," said Coral. "Tell them I will be down in just a moment."

"Very good, miss." The maid scurried away.

Coral waited until she was gone and then went down the hall and used the toilet. She returned to her room, dressed, put her hair up, and then looked at herself in the mirror. She looked slightly different to herself: older, and perhaps a little harder.

That's her," Coral heard a voice say as she rounded the bend in the staircase.

Mrs Raleigh and the policeman were standing at the bottom of the stairs.

The policeman held out his hand. "Miss Glynn? How do you do? I'm Inspector Hoke."

She shook his hand. "Good morning," she said. "Good morning, Mrs Raleigh."

"Yes," said Mrs Raleigh, agreeing with, rather than reciprocating, the greeting.

"Is Major Hart here?" Coral asked.

"No," said Inspector Hoke. "I have arranged to speak with him later this morning at Hart House. But I shall take this opportunity to speak with you alone, Miss Glynn. Surely you have no objection to that?"

"No," said Coral. "None at all."

"Very well. If you'll follow me, Mrs Raleigh has kindly allowed us to use her office." He indicated an open door behind the reception desk.

Coral, who assumed all official people spoke literally, did not move.

"After you," he said.

"Oh," she said. "I'm sorry. You said to follow you . . ."

"Merely a figure of speech," he said. "Ladies first."

She entered the tiny office and stood while he came in behind her and closed the door.

"Please sit," he said. He indicated the one chair behind the desk; the office was too small to accommodate any others.

"I think I would prefer to stand," she said.

"As you wish, Miss Glynn. Now, I would simply like to ask you a few questions. As you no doubt have heard, a young girl was found murdered in the Sap Green Forest."

"How do you know it was murder?"

"I beg your pardon?"

"Wasn't she hanged?" asked Coral.

"Yes, she was."

"Then couldn't it have been suicide?"

"No. Definitely not. We know it was murder."

"How?"

"The evidence, the circumstances . . . I can be no more specific than that, I'm afraid. And five-year-old girls rarely take their own lives."

"I see," said Coral.

"She was found at a spot in the woods not far from Hart House. I understand you have been living there for some time?"

"Yes," said Coral. "Until very recently."

"How long have you been here, at the Swan?"

"Four or five days," said Coral. "Since Monday."

"May I ask why?"

"I am engaged to marry Major Hart, so of course we must live apart until the wedding."

"Of course. And when will that be?"

"Next Saturday, I believe."

"So soon! May I ask why?"

"We are eager to be married. We see no need to wait."

"For how long have you been engaged?"

"A week—or two."

"Can you be more precise, Miss Glynn?"

"Certainly, although I hardly see how it could matter. It was the day Mrs Hart died—no, the following day."

"And how long have you known Major Hart?"

"What has that got to do with the girl in the woods?"

"These questions may seem odd to you, Miss Glynn—impolite, in fact—but I assure you that I must ask them. You are free to be silent if you prefer. I assume you have nothing to hide. Perhaps I am mistaken."

"Of course I do not. I only wonder why you ask them."

"You are a newcomer to our community, Miss Glynn. I am only trying to acquaint ourselves. Did you know Major Hart before you arrived at Hart House?"

"No."

"And when was that?"

"I was there for about a month before Mrs Hart died."

"Do you remember the date of your arrival?"

"It was the nineteenth of March."

"And I assume you met Major Hart soon thereafter?"

"Yes. That same evening."

"Very good. I understand you are a walker, Miss Glynn. Is that correct?"

"A walker?"

"Yes."

"I'm not sure what you mean."

"I understand that you enjoy taking walks."

"As much as anyone, I suppose."

"Really? Mrs Prence told me you often went for walks."

"Did she?"

"Indeed she did. She said you often walked in the Sap Green Forest."

"I would not say often. Several times, perhaps."

"Do you remember how many times?"

"Three or four times," said Coral. "No more than that."

"And given your abbreviated tenure at Hart House, would you not consider that often?"

"No, I would not. Occasional, perhaps, but not often."

"Can you tell me, Miss Glynn, on these occasional walks of yours, did you see anyone or anything that appeared strange to you?"

"Strange?"

"Yes, strange. Out of the ordinary."

"It would be hard for me to say what was ordinary in the woods, as I was unfamiliar with them."

"I see your point. Did you see anyone while you were walking in the woods? Or near to them?"

Coral paused for a moment. "No," she said. "I did not."

"No one?"

"No one that I remember," said Coral. "A dog, perhaps."

"You saw a dog?"

"I said perhaps. Perhaps I saw a dog."

"Very well. I have only a few more questions. For how long have you worked as a privately hired nurse, Miss Glynn?"

"Just a few years," she said. "Since '48."

"I see. And how many patients, would you say, have you nursed in that time?"

"Oh, I don't know. Perhaps six a year. Fifteen, sixteen, something like that."

"And can you tell me, Miss Glynn, how many of those patients have died while receiving your care?"

"Well, all of the terminal patients have died. That is to be expected of terminal patients."

"Like Mrs Hart?"

"Yes," said Coral. "She was a terminal patient."

"Have you nursed any nonterminal patients, Miss Glynn?"

"Yes, I have. Several."

"And have any of those patients died while being nursed by you?"

"No," said Coral. "None. I am happy to tell you that they recovered."

"And I am so happy to hear it," said Inspector Hoke. "I am sure you are a very fine nurse."

"I try my best to be," said Coral.

"Well, I have no more questions for you at the present time, and I thank you very much for answering the ones I've asked. You've been most cooperative, Miss Glynn. Thank you so much."

"You're welcome."

The Inspector opened the door and motioned for her to pass through. "Ladies first," he said, and smiled. "Oh, Miss Glynn . . ." he said as she passed him by.

"Yes?" She paused just outside the door.

"Will you and the Major be taking a wedding trip?"

"No," said Coral. "At least, we have not planned one."

"So you will be residing at Hart House after the wedding?"

"Yes, I will. We will."

"Very good. I just want to make sure I know where to find you. If you do plan a wedding trip, please be certain to let me know. Is that asking too much?"

"We have no trip planned," said Coral.

"You'd best wait for the summer weather," he said, "and then take a proper holiday."

•

She had breakfast in the dining room and then sat in the lounge, looking at pictures of horses in hunting magazines until she was sure the shops would be open.

Her entrance into Dalrymple's Better Dresses was identical to the entrance she had made the previous morning: the bell jangled, the beads parted, and Mrs Henderson appeared. It was like stepping backwards, or sideways, in time.

"Oh," Mrs Henderson said. "Good morning."

"Good morning," said Coral. "I am sorry about all the trouble yesterday."

"Do you want the dress or not?"

"I said I was sorry about the trouble."

"I am very sorry about it all as well."

"I would like the dress," said Coral. "I am getting married after all. There was just some difficulty yesterday . . ."

"Jitters," said Mrs Henderson. "There are always jitters! They are a part of any wedding, my dear. I, myself, suffered terrible jitters when marrying Mr Henderson. I required a sedatival injection."

"Can the dress be mended?" asked Coral. "I did not mean to tear it."

"Of course you did not. You should not have attempted to put it on by yourself. I have already mended the seam. It is as good as new. Shall I wrap it up for you?"

"You needn't do the box and everything," said Coral.

"Nonsense! A dress does not leave Dalrymple's without a box. I will have it ready for you in one moment."

Mrs Henderson parted the beads and disappeared into the backroom. Coral sat on the pouf at the centre of the room and looked out the front window into the High Street. Across the road, the sign in front of the newsagent's read:

## HANGED GIRL DEFILED?
## MURDERER STILL AT LARGE

After a moment Mrs Henderson emerged with a box identical to the one she had presented to Coral the previous day.

"I hope you will be very happy in this beautiful dress, my dear. And if your jitters return, there is nothing more soothing than a hot bath and a glass of sherry. Enjoyed simultaneously, if possible."

"Will you come to our wedding luncheon?" asked Coral.

"Your wedding luncheon!"

"It is on Saturday, at the Black Swan. It would mean so much to me for you to be there. You have been very kind to me, and I have no family or friends here . . ."

"Oh, you poor dear thing!" exclaimed Mrs Henderson. "Of course I shall come. I am moved beyond words. You say you have no family here?"

"I have no family anywhere," said Coral.

"You poor child! It is too, too sad. But I have felt like your mother since the moment you first stepped in the door! That is why I found the unpleasantness so upsetting. Don't move, my dear! I shall return in a flash!"

Mrs Henderson dove back through the beaded curtain and emerged a moment later with a small box wrapped in gold paper. "This is for you, my dear. A present for you—silk stockings, which have just arrived from Paris. You must wear them on Saturday with your dress. Silk, my dear, real silk!"

"Oh, I couldn't accept them," said Coral. "You're too kind. It isn't right."

"Of course it's right. I do not do wrong things. Take them and don't say another word. Will you need help with the dress on Saturday?"

"A friend of Major Hart's will help me, I think."

"Well, if you need anything, or anyone, you must let me know.

I will be there in a thrice. I'm so happy this has all worked out so
nicely. I do so hate any unpleasantness where dresses are concerned."

"Yes," said Coral. "So do I."

"Well, until Saturday, then. There's nothing else you need—
hat, gloves, shoes?"

"I am ready," said Coral.

"And no more jitters!" cried Mrs Henderson. "I forbid them!"
She leant forwards and embraced Coral. Coral felt her face pressed
against Mrs Henderson's plush bosom, smelt lavender and talc. Her
own mother had not been the coddling kind, and physical affection—
any affection, for that matter—was mysterious to her, like hearing
foreigners speak their own language. She remembered how the man,
the one with the rubber Johnny, had collapsed on top of her when he
had depleted himself and mashed his wet mouth into her neck, like
someone trying to eat something in the dark, rocking his body against
hers like something being wound down; how he started to weep, all
the while rocking, mouthing her neck, moaning, the juice leaking out
of the rubber Johnny that shrivelled off his wilted penis, the cold, ugly
dampness of his fluid on her thighs.

She clung for a moment to Mrs Henderson and then turned
and hurried out the door, setting the bell pealing once again.


This is my mother, Florence Coppard," Dolly announced when the
two women had managed to squeeze themselves into Coral's tiny
room. "A marriage won't be happy unless there's weeping at the
wedding, and Mother is a great weeper. You'll weep, won't you,
Mother? You'll weep for Coral?"

"Yes, of course," said Dolly's mother. "I always weep at wed-
dings."

"This isn't a church wedding, Mrs Coppard," said Coral,
who worried that Dolly's mother's sentimentality might be site-
specific.

"Oh, it doesn't matter," said Dolly. "She'll weep anywhere. Won't you, Mother?"

Mrs Coppard allowed that she would, and said to call her Flossie.

"Sit down, Mother, over there on the bed, and stay out of the way." Dolly pushed her mother towards the bed and turned towards Coral. "Now, have you bathed? What are you planning to do with your hair? Where's your dress?"

"It's in the wardrobe," said Coral, electing to answer only one of Dolly's many questions.

"Now, before we start, do you need a tipple, darling? You're shaking like a leaf. Nerves! Have you got your flask in your bag, Mother?"

"Course I have." Mrs Coppard opened her bag and withdrew a silver flask, which she handed to her daughter.

Dolly unscrewed the cap, which was attached to the bottle with a thin silver chain, and held it towards Coral.

"No, thank you," said Coral.

"You haven't got nerves! I've got nerves, and I'm only the bridesmaid."

"The witness," said Coral.

"It's the same thing," said Dolly. "Have a tipple."

"I'm fine," said Coral. "I just need help doing up the dress."

"Would you like a tipple, Mother?"

"I might as well," said Mrs Coppard, reaching out for the flask. She took a dainty sip and then stowed the flask back in her bag.

"Time for the dress!" announced Dolly. "It's in here?" She indicated the wardrobe.

"Yes," said Coral.

Dolly opened the wardrobe. "Oh, you shouldn't have hung it on such a cheap hanger. Look, Mother, she's hung her lovely wedding dress on a cheap hanger."

"Well, it's her dress, my dear. I suppose she can do whatever she wants with it."

"Oh, Coral, it's beautiful!" exclaimed Dolly. "It isn't the one I thought at all."

Coral opened the top drawer of the dresser and removed the small package wrapped in gold paper. "I've got these as well," she timidly said.

"Got what?" asked Dolly.

"Stockings," said Coral. "Mrs Henderson gave them to me. As a gift. They're silk."

"Silk! Real silk?"

"Yes," said Coral. "From Paris."

"I suppose she wants to get on your good side," said Dolly, "seeing how you're marrying Clement. She thinks you'll be buying lots of dresses and doesn't want you going up to London for them."

"I invited her to the luncheon," said Coral.

"Mrs Henderson?"

"Yes. And the boy at the flower shop."

"Does Clement know you invited them?"

"Yes," said Coral. "He said I might invite whomever I wanted. Since he invited you and Robin."

"Well, we're your witnesses, darling, of course we're invited to the luncheon. It's not even a question of inviting. But it's a bit odd to invite tradespeople, wouldn't you agree?"

"It might seem odd to you," said Coral, "but it is not odd to me."

"Well, fancy Mrs Henderson making you a gift of silk stockings. Perhaps it's a tradition. What's the poem, Mother? 'Something bothered, something blue, a wedding gift from me to you'?"

"I don't think that's quite it," said Mrs Coppard. "It's certainly not 'bothered.' Why would you give a bride something bothered?"

"Words meant different things back then," explained Dolly. "Like 'cudgel.'"

"Cudgel? What's cudgel?"

"It used to be a fish, I think. Some sort of eel. But now it's something else. Or now it's an eel and before it was something else. Words change. 'Bothered' used to mean something handmade, I think. Something you bothered over."

"I think it's 'borrowed,'" said Mrs Coppard.

"It's not," said Dolly. "It's bothered. 'Borrowed' makes no sense at all. You can't give something borrowed."

"I don't see why not," said Mrs Coppard.

"Why must you always contradict me, Mother?"

"I don't always contradict you, my dear, only often, and that's because you're so often wrong." Mrs Coppard opened her bag and rummaged in it, extracting the flask.

"No more tipples, Mother, it makes you disagreeable."

"Those who speak the truth are always thought disagreeable," philosophised Mrs Coppard. She helped herself and then held the flask out towards Coral. "Tempt you, my dear?" she asked.

"She doesn't want any!" cried Dolly. "Put it away, Mother, and sit quietly, or we'll send you down to the lounge."

"At least I could get a proper drink down there."

"No you couldn't," said Dolly, "since the bar doesn't open until noon."

Coral, who saw no end to this discussion, said, "Perhaps it would be better."

"What?" asked Dolly. "Perhaps what?"

"If your mother— It's only that it's a tiny room, and with all of us in it . . . perhaps it would be better if she went down to the lounge. I'm sure they'd give her a drink if she asked."

"Of course, darling," said Dolly. "Did you hear that, Mother? Coral wants you to go down to the lounge. It's too crowded in here."

"No, it's not that—it's just that I thought she might be more comfortable . . ."

"Don't say another word," said Mrs Coppard. "It wasn't my idea to come. Dolly thought that as you hadn't got a mother, I might be a comfort to you, but if I'm in your way, I'll make myself scarce."

"It was lovely of you to come, Mrs Coppard, it's only that I'd like to be alone with Dolly for a moment."

It took awhile for Mrs Coppard to arise and collect her things, as she had settled herself quite completely upon the bed. When she had righted and reassembled herself, she kissed Coral and said, "I wish you all the happiness in the world, my dear," and left the room.

As soon as she was gone, Coral held her hands to her face and began to cry.

"Darling!" said Dolly. "What's wrong? Sit down here on the bed. Go on, sit." She pushed Coral towards the bed and then down upon it, and sat beside her. "What's wrong, darling? Do you want a tipple? Should I go get Mother's flask?"

Coral shook her head and then wiped the tears away from her eyes with her hands. "Oh, Dolly!" she cried.

"What? What is it, Coral? Tell me, darling."

"I don't know what to do," said Coral.

"Do you have doubts, darling? Jitters? Every girl has them. You oughtn't worry, even if it does all seem too ghastly for words, I promise you it isn't at all—"

"No," said Coral. "It isn't that."

"Then what is it, darling? Tell me."

"I'm worried that I am—not in a position to marry Major Hart."

"Whatever do you mean? Do you mean because of class? None of that matters anymore, darling. And Clement had quite given up on marrying any girl at all, you see, so—"

"No," said Coral. "It isn't that."

"Then whatever is it?"

"I'm with child," said Coral.

"Coral! Whatever do you mean? Do you mean that you are pregnant?"

"Yes," said Coral. "And I don't know what to do . . ."

"But whose . . . Is it Clement's? Don't tell me he's . . . or that you've—"

"No," said Coral. "It isn't his. It can't possibly be."

"Then whose is it? Have you got a beau somewhere?"

"No," said Coral. "At my previous position—it was with a family; the children had scarlet fever, all three of them, and they needed a nurse, and the husband—"

"Oh, darling—did he force himself upon you?"

"Yes," said Coral.

"Oh, how awful," said Dolly. "You poor thing. Aren't men brutes? I'm so lucky with Robin, I forget how horrible most men are, as bad as dogs—"

"What can I do?" asked Coral. "What should I do?"

"Well, that depends," said Dolly. "First of all, you mustn't cry. Men can always tell when women have been crying, I expect because they're so often the cause of it. Let me get you a hankie."

Dolly opened her bag and extracted a handkerchief. She handed it to Coral and watched Coral dab at her eyes and blow her nose and then said, "How far gone are you?"

"About three months," said Coral.

"Do you want to get rid of it?"

"I don't know," said Coral. "I don't know what to do . . ."

"Couldn't you do it yourself? You are a nurse, after all."

"I suppose," said Coral, "but it's dangerous."

"I know a girl who got one, and she was fine," said Dolly. "She just wept all the time."

"Do you know someone who—"

"Oh, darling, forget about all that. Just marry him, marry Clement and it will all be fine. Everyone will think it's his, and perhaps he will, too. Men are so stupid about babies."

"You don't think I should tell him?"

"Tell him? Of course not! Just go ahead with everything, marry him, and it will all work itself out."

"But what if he finds out?"

"People don't find out things they'd rather not. And if he does, you'll be married and there's nothing he can do about it without embarrassing himself."

"You're sure I shouldn't tell him?" asked Coral.

"I've never been surer of anything," said Dolly. "Trust me, darling. Just put it all out of your mind. Oh, you poor dear. Really, you mustn't let anything ruin your happy occasion. We get so little happiness in life, you know."

They sat in silence for a moment and then Coral stood. "If you'll help me Dolly, I'll put on the dress."

"Of course!" said Dolly. "That is what I am here for, darling. Now, have you got new under things?"

"No," said Coral. "Just the dress and stockings."

"Oh, darling, you should have new under things—"

"It's all right," said Coral. "I don't need them. I only need—"

The door was knocked upon and Dolly called out, "Who is it?"

"It's me, ma'am," said the maid. "Major Hart and Mr. Lofting are downstairs. They say it is time for you to go."

"Tell them we'll be there in a moment!" Dolly shouted at the door.

There was no weeping at the wedding. The car Major Hart had hired could only accommodate the four members of the bridal party, so Mrs Coppard stayed behind at The Black Swan to supervise the preparations for the wedding luncheon. And perhaps, even if Mrs Coppard had accompanied the bridal party to the magistrate's office, she might not have shed a single tear, for there was nothing sentimental or lovely about the ceremony. Sensing this deficiency and feeling short-changed, Dolly asked if she might sing "Two Roses in a Garden Grew," but the magistrate would not allow it, and so the ceremony remained unadorned by feeling.

An awkward scene awaited the bridal party back at The Black Swan, where Major Hart had reserved a private dining room for their luncheon. It was a problem of size: the room was too large. It contained a long rectangular table set for sixteen, with seven places down each side and one at either end. Mrs Coppard, had, in the absence of any other suitable hostess, taken it upon herself to arrange the seating, and had put Mrs Prence, Mrs Henderson, and the pansy from the flower shop along one side with two empty places on either side of Mrs Henderson. She suggested that Robin and Dolly sit at the far ends of the other side, Robin next to the bride at one end and Dolly next to the groom at the other. She would take the middle seat, opposite Mrs Henderson.

Mrs Henderson, who felt stranded in the middle of the table with only Mrs Coppard directly across from her for company, said, "Perhaps it would be jollier if we cleared away the extra settings and shifted everyone down towards one end of the table?"

"Oh, no," said Mrs Coppard. "That would never do. It's a wedding luncheon, so the bride and groom must have the seats of honour."

"Perhaps they could sit beside each other at one end, and we could group ourselves about them," suggested Mrs Henderson. "That would be more convivial, and then we needn't shout to each other."

"There is no need for anyone to shout," said Mrs Coppard. "I think this arrangement suits us fine. And it will do nicely for the photographs, instead of us all lumped up together."

Mrs Henderson resigned herself to the trial the luncheon had quickly become and said no more. The bridal party arrived, and when they were all correspondingly seated, a waiter appeared with a magnum of champagne and went round the table, filling everyone's *coupe*. He was young and terrified and had apparently been told that each squat glass must be filled to its brim. Everyone sat in silence while this feat was slowly and painstakingly achieved. Little beads of quivering perspiration appeared on the waiter's forehead. Watching him was like watching a medical student suture a wound.

When the waiter had scurried out of the room, Robin stood and attempted to raise his glass, but its brimming abundance made this impossible, so he bent down and sipped preventively from it and, so tamed, managed to hold it before him. "A toast," he said, "to Clement and Coral: May their days be long and their loads be light, with peaceful days and fruitful nights!"

Everyone agreed to this toast by leaning over and sipping in a delicate feline way at their champagne. No one dared to raise his or her glass. When Clement sat down, Dolly popped up as if some sort of valve connected them. "I tried to sing this song at the ceremony but the magistrate thought he was too good for it, so I shall sing for you all now. Mother, have you got your pitch pipe?"

"I know I put it in here," said Mrs Coppard. She picked her bag off the floor and rummaged through it, extracting a brush, a banana, the flask, and eventually a pitch pipe, which she held to her lips.

"C major," Dolly said.

"I know," said Mrs Coppard, "just let me find it." She found and blew the pitch and Dolly began to sing "Two Roses in a Garden Grew." As she was the kind of singer who riveted attention upon herself, no one noticed that during her song the door had quietly opened and Inspector Hoke stepped into the private dining room. He, too, appeared to be raptly entranced by Dolly's performance and was the only one who applauded its conclusion. This had the effect of diverting everyone's attention away from Dolly and onto himself.

"Brava, Mrs Lofting!" he said. "A beautiful song, beautifully sung, by a beautiful woman."

It was odd that it was Coral, not Major Hart, who stood up. "What do you want?" she asked Inspector Hoke.

"Ah, Miss Glynn," he said. "Although I suppose by now it is Mrs Hart, isn't it? Congratulations."

"What is it you want?" asked Coral.

"Just a word with you, if you would be so kind."

Major Hart stood up then and said, "What's this about, Hoke? We've just been married, for God's sake."

"A thousand pardons, Major Hart, and a thousand good wishes to you and your bride. Perhaps we might have a private word in the corridor?"

"Certainly not," said the Major. He walked the length of the table and put his arms on Coral's shoulders. "Sit, my dear," he told her. "This is our wedding day, Hoke. It is neither the time nor the place for your interference."

"It was only a brief word that I wanted," said the Inspector.

"Then come to us tomorrow, at Hart House, as you should have originally done," said Major Hart. "We shall be available to speak with you then."

"I'm afraid I cannot wait that long," said Inspector Hoke. "I know the timing is unfortunate but I must speak with Miss Glynn—Mrs Hart—today."

"This evening, then," said the Major. "Five o'clock."

"Very well," said the Inspector. "I am sorry to have interrupted your party. Sometimes the duties of a policeman are unpleasant."

"No doubt," said Major Hart. "We'll see you this evening."

When the Inspector had withdrawn and closed the door behind him, Major Hart returned to his place and picked up his glass of champagne. "I ask you all to stand and make a toast to my beautiful wife."

Everyone stood and raised his or her glass of champagne.

Major Hart said, "I had resigned myself to being alone in my life, and miserable. I wish to toast the woman who has changed all of that—the woman whom I love, and to whom I am forever indebted. To Coral!"

"To Coral!" everyone echoed, and this time they were able to raise their glasses and drink heartily from them.

Mrs Prence brought their tea into the library and lay the tray on the low table in front of the fire. "Thank you, Mary," Major Hart said from behind the scrim of his newspaper. He had already thrown the first page into the fire, where the flames had hungrily devoured the headline:

## CLUES FOUND IN SAP GREEN FOREST
### POLICE CLOSING IN

Mrs Prence stepped away from the table and stood there for a moment, apparently at her wit's end. When it became clear that the Major was not aware of her continuing presence, she cleared her throat and said, "Excuse me, sir."

Major Hart folded his paper onto his lap and said, "What is it, Mary?"

"I'm not one for toasts," said Mrs Prence. "Not like those others at the luncheon. Or songs, for that matter. But I did want to say, sir, to you and Mrs Hart, that I wish you a very happy life together."

"That's very kind of you to say, Mary," said the Major. "Isn't it, Coral?"

"Yes," said Coral. "Thank you, Mrs Prence."

"This is for you, ma'am," said Mrs Prence. She took a little cloisonné box off the tea tray and handed it to Coral.

"Oh, Mrs Prence," said Coral. "I couldn't accept it."

"Don't be silly, Coral," said the Major. "Of course you may."

"It's very sweet," said Coral. "And I love little boxes."

"The gift is inside," said Mrs Prence. "Along with the box, of course. Open it."

Coral unscrewed the top off the box. Inside of it lay a pair of garish gold and ruby earrings. "Oh, they're beautiful!" she exclaimed.

"Very pretty," said Major Hart.

"They belonged to my grandmother," explained Mrs Prence. "My mother's mother. She had a bit of Gypsy blood in her and did like pretty things. Them's real rubies, she always claimed, although they could be just bits of coloured glass, I suppose."

"Oh, but if they belonged to your grandmother, you should keep them," said Coral. "They're heirlooms."

"They're no use to me," said Mrs Prence. "I wouldn't pierce my ears for all the tea in China, nor would I wear them if I did. But I thought they might suit you very well, ma'am."

Coral thought it would be churlish to point out that her ears were also unpierced. "Well, they're very pretty and I shall treasure them," she said, tucking them back into the little box. "Thank you."

"Very kind of you, Mary," said the Major. "Will you join us for a cup of tea?"

"Oh, no, sir. I've got the supper to make. I thought after that big stuffing luncheon, my egg and cheese ramekins might be nice?"

"Splendid," said the Major. "Will you pour, Coral?"

Mrs Prence left the room and the Major disappeared behind his newspaper. Coral poured tea into the cups and then realised she had not the least idea how the Major took his tea. It seemed a strange question to ask one's husband, and it made her think of everything else she didn't know about him—or rather, how very little she did know. There he sat across from her, close enough to touch. It would come to that soon enough, she thought. Tonight. In the huge old canopied bed his mother had so recently died in. She had been shocked when he told her this was to be their room; she had imagined that its door would be closed and never reopened, the room and its contents forgotten. But of course it was the master bedroom. There was a new quilted coverlet on the bed, and yet, the old lady's clothes still hung in the wardrobes, and her ancient under things lay perennially undisturbed, like hard-packed drifts of snow, in the bureau drawers.

"How do you like your tea?" she asked her husband.

He poked his head around the edge of the newspaper and said, "What?"

"Your tea. How do you like it?"

"Ah," he said. "Milk, no sugar, please."

She dripped milk into one of the cups of tea and handed it to him.

"Many thanks," he said. He put the saucer down on the table

and reopened the newspaper before him. She sipped her tea and looked around the room. I live here now, she thought. All of this is mine. But it made no sense, it was like thinking that Timbuktu was hers. She was sure she would always feel a foreigner here. But then, she had never felt at home anywhere. In the past few years her itinerant nursing had made her an interloper in one home after another, arriving in each home along with the damp stain of sickness or the dark shadow of death, an unwelcome but necessary guest, tolerated but never embraced. So it was impossible for Coral to imagine sitting in a room and not feeling imposed upon it.

When the Major had finished his tea, she lifted the pot and said, "More?"

"Is it still warm?" he asked.

The pot felt only faintly warm. "Not very," she said. "Would you like a fresh pot?"

"No," he said. "What time is it? Perhaps I'll have a drink." He looked at his watch. "It's almost five," he said. "That damned Hoke will be here any minute."

Coral stood and picked up the tray.

"Leave that," he said. "Mrs Prence will clear it all away."

"I'd like to go down and have a word with her," said Coral.

"Awfully nice of her to give you that jewellry. And speaking of which, I have to get you a ring, haven't I?"

"You don't have to."

"Of course I do. You're a married lady. You must wear a ring."

"What about you? Shouldn't you have one as well?"

"Oh, it's different for men," he said. "I've got this ring." He showed her the signet ring on his pinkie finger. "It was my father's. That's all the jewellry I want. We'll have to go into town—there's a decent jeweller's there, I believe. Or perhaps you'd like Mother's band? Of course it's all yours now, her jewellry."

"I think if I am to wear a ring, I would like it to be my own."

"Of course," he said. "We'll go to town on Monday."

•

Mrs Prence was beating eggs with barely suppressed fury when Coral appeared in the kitchen with the tea tray.

"You had only need ring," she said, "and I would have come up for it."

"I know," said Coral. "But I wanted to come down. And thank you for the lovely gift. It was very kind of you. And I wanted to say . . . that I am sorry about before, about the unpleasantness between us."

"I'm sure it is a thing of the past," said Mrs Prence.

"Yes. I know that this is your home," said Coral, "and I want you to be happy here. I want you to go on doing things as you always have—unless, of course, there are changes you would like to make. I don't pretend to have any experience running a house. But if there is anything I can do to help you, please let me know."

"I'm sure I can manage. I always have."

They heard the bell at the front door.

"Who can that be?" asked Mrs Prence.

"It's probably Inspector Hoke," said Coral.

"Ah, yes," said Mrs Prence. "He wants to talk to you about that nasty business in the woods, doesn't he?"

"Yes," said Coral.

"You mustn't be afraid of him," said Mrs Prence. "He is a very kind man. If you have nothing to hide, you must tell him everything you know."

"Of course I will," said Coral.

Inspector Hoke was shaking rain from his coat in the front hall when Coral emerged from the kitchen. Major Hart was standing nearby, looking vacant.

"Let me hang that up for you, Inspector Hoke," Coral said. She opened the closet door and withdrew a hanger.

"Thank you kindly," said the Inspector, "but it's a bit damp. I'll spare you the trouble." He took the hanger from her and fitted it into his coat, then hung it in the closet, shifting the coats nearest to it away. He closed the closet door and brushed his hands together. "Good evening, Mrs Hart. My apologies for interrupting your luncheon this afternoon. I trust that it proceeded merrily?"

"Yes, thank you," said Coral.

"Now, where could we sit and chat for a moment?"

"There is a fire in the library," said Coral, and indicated the open door.

They all three entered the library. The Inspector and Coral sat and the Major stood beside the drinks cart. "I was just about to make myself a drink," he said. "Would you like something, Inspector?"

"Thank you, but no."

"Darling?"

"A little brandy, perhaps."

"Of course." The Major poured brandy into one glass and some whiskey into another and sat on the couch beside his wife, facing the fire. "Well," he said to the Inspector, "what is this all about?"

"It's good of you to make time for me on this day of all days," said the Inspector.

"This is about the girl in the woods I assume?" asked the Major.

"Yes," said the Inspector. "Some evidence has been discovered that warrants me speaking to you again. It is actually you, Mrs Hart, I wish to speak with."

"Evidence? What kind of evidence?" asked the Major.

"I'll get to that in a moment, Major. I would prefer to speak with Mrs Hart alone, if that is all right with you."

"It certainly isn't," said the Major.

"It is really up to you, Mrs Hart. Would you prefer to speak with me alone?"

"I would not," said Coral.

"Very well," said the Inspector. "When I spoke with you last,

Mrs Hart, you told me that you often walked in the Sap Green Forest."

"I said that I had walked several times in the forest."

"Forgive me, I now remember your making that distinction. And if I remember correctly, you also told me that you saw no one walking in or near the woods."

"Yes," said Coral. "That is correct."

"Tell me, Mrs Hart, when you made these several walks, did you remain on the pathways, or did you venture from them?"

"I think I stayed mostly to the pathways."

"Never venturing from them?"

"Not that I remember."

"But you allow the possibility that you ventured from the path?"

"Look here, Hoke, what are you getting at? I wish you'd stop with all this detective nonsense."

"It is not nonsense, Major. Please allow me to proceed."

"Well, if you've got something to say, I wish you'd just say it, and stop with all these damned ridiculous questions."

"Mrs Hart, there is a large coppice of holly trees in the forest. Do you remember seeing them on any of your walks?

"Yes," she said, "I do."

"And did you venture into them?"

"Into them? No."

"You are sure?"

"Yes," said Coral. "I remember stopping near to them, but that is all."

"Why did you stop?"

"Because I heard something, a noise coming from them."

"What kind of a noise?"

"At first I thought it might be an animal. But then, as I listened, I realised it was only the sound of the holly leaves rubbing against themselves. They make a strange sound."

The Inspector reached into his jacket and pulled a little cloth pouch from its inner pocket. He loosened the strings holding the pouch closed and shook it. A button fell onto the table, spun on its axis for a moment, and then lay still. It was made of butterscotch Bakelite, rather ordinary, of medium size.

"Do you recognise this button?" Inspector Hoke asked Coral.

Coral said nothing. She looked at the button and then bent forwards and touched it with one of her fingers, flipping it over.

"Where did you find it?" she asked.

"So you recognise it?"

"Yes," said Coral. "It is from the sleeve of my coat."

"Yes," said the Inspector. "I noticed you were missing a button when I hung up my coat."

"How clever you are," said Coral. "Where did you find it?"

"It was found in the Sap Green Forest. Deep within the stand of holly, very near to where the little girl was hanged. I ask you again, Mrs Hart, and for the final time, did you venture into the holly? Did you see anyone when you walked in the forest?"

"Look here, Hoke," said the Major. "I don't know what you're getting at, but you can't go about insulting my wife like that. She'll answer no more of your questions until we've consulted our solicitor."

"No," said Coral. "The Inspector is right. It is time I told him the truth."

"You needn't tell him anything, darling—"

"I saw the holly," Coral said, "as I told you. And I heard that strange sound coming from it. At first I did think it was wind rubbing the leaves, but then I realised it wasn't the wind, it was something—a person or an animal—crying out. So I pushed into the holly, and it was difficult, because it is grows so densely, but I found a little passage—a tunnel almost—and followed that into a small clearing in the centre."

She stopped speaking for a moment and gazed into the fire.

"It was two children," she continued, "a boy and girl. The girl was tied up by her wrists, hanging from a branch, and the boy was throwing pinecones and sticks at her. I asked them what they were doing and they told me they were playing a game: Prisoner. And I told them it wasn't a nice game and they should stop playing it at once. And they said they liked it; that they took turns being prisoner. I tried to untie the girl but the knots were too tight. And I didn't know what else I could do. What could I do? So I told them to be careful and left them."

"And you told no one about what you had seen?" asked the Inspector.

"No," said Coral. "I knew no one; I forgot about it."

"How could you forget such a scene? Were you not worried for the little girl?"

"Yes," said Coral. "Of course. But I forgot. I was preoccupied. It was the day that Major Hart had asked me to marry him, and I had promised to give him an answer that evening, and so—I forgot . . ."

"Was the little girl injured when you saw her?"

"Yes," said Coral. "Well, not really injured. She had some abrasions on her face." Coral touched her cheek.

"You saw a young girl tied up and tortured in the woods and you said or did nothing about it?"

"Yes," said Coral. "I told you—"

"But, Coral, why?" asked the Major.

She looked at him. "I meant to, I suppose. Or perhaps I felt guilty because I hadn't stopped them. But I tried to! I was frightened by them, I think. There was something frightening about it all."

"You were scared of a little boy?

"He wasn't so little," said Coral.

"How old was he?"

"I don't know," said Coral. "Maybe ten, eleven . . ."

"A little boy," said the Inspector.

"Yes," said Coral. "I suppose. But I was in such a muddle myself, you see, it didn't really register. It was wrong of me, I know, but I couldn't think about it . . ."

"I'm afraid that there is another matter," said the Inspector, "that I must speak with you about."

Coral thought the Major might once again interfere on her behalf, but this time he did not. He was slumped back into the sofa's cushions, watching the fire, as if Coral and the Inspector were chatting friends who bored him.

"What is that?" she asked.

"It concerns the circumstances of your prior employment. Actually, the circumstances that ended your prior employment."

"There was a misunderstanding there," said Coral. "Several, in fact."

"Misunderstandings?"

"Yes," said Coral. "Misunderstandings. And unpleasantness."

"I spoke with Mrs Rosalind DeVries. She was your last employer, correct?"

"Yes. I nursed her children."

"She told me that you stole something from her. A ring."

"I did not steal it. It was a misunderstanding."

"She said she found her ring in one of your bags."

"I had found it," said Coral.

"And you knew it belonged to Mrs DeVries?"

"Yes."

"Then why did you not return it to her?"

"I planned to do that—when she had noticed it missing."

"And if she had not noticed it was missing?"

"I would have given it back to her. I am not a thief."

"I'm sorry, but it sounds as if you are. Taking something that doesn't belong to you and having it in your possession is thievery."

"I didn't take it," said Coral. "I found it."

"It hardly matters in this case," said the Inspector. "You are very lucky they did not charge you."

"That was not all," said Coral. "There was more unpleasantness in that house."

"What do you mean?"

"Her husband—Mr DeVries—was unpleasant to me."

"I'm not surprised, if you stole his wife's ring."

"I do not mean that kind of unpleasantness," said Coral.

"Oh," said the Inspector. "What do you mean?"

"He was physically unpleasant to me," said Coral. "He forced himself upon me."

The Major cleared his throat.

"Do you mean to say that he molested you?" asked the Inspector.

"Yes," said Coral.

"Did you tell the police?"

"No."

"Did you tell Mrs DeVries?"

"She would not have believed me. She thought me a thief."

"But you were a thief."

"I was not. I told you I was not."

"Well, that is all in the past. It need not concern us. You are well away from there, at any event. But what you saw in the Sap Green Forest—that is not the past; that is what concerns me."

"It is the past," said Coral.

"Beg pardon?"

"What happened in the woods—the girl—that is the past."

"It may have happened in the past, but it still under investigation. That was the distinction I was making. It is the matter at hand. Not the unpleasantness with the DeVrieses."

"Then why did you mention it?" asked Coral.

"Because it has bearing on your character," said the Inspector, "and your trustworthiness."

"But what of his character?"

"Whose?"

"Mr DeVries!"

"I make no judgement of his character whatsoever."

"Even after what I told you he did to me?"

"It is beyond my purview. If what you say is true, he is a loath-some creature. But his character has no bearing on the matter at hand."

"And mine does?"

"Have you told me the truth—the complete truth—about what you saw in the Sap Green Forest, Mrs Hart?"

"Yes," she said, "I have."

"There is nothing you can, or wish, to add?"

"No," said Coral. "Only that—"

"What?"

"That I am sorry. Sorry that I did not speak to someone about what I saw. But I knew no one—"

"You said Major Hart proposed marriage to you that very day. Did you not know him?"

Coral looked at the Major. She shook her head. "No," she said. "Not really."

The Major reached out and took her hand. "Our courtship was brief," he said.

"Yes, I gathered as much," said the Inspector. He stood up. "Perhaps I could have a word with you in the hallway, Major. Privately. You'll excuse us, won't you, Mrs Hart?"

"Of course," said Coral.

The Inspector opened the door and followed the Major out into the hallway, closing the door behind them.

"I'm sorry about all this," he said to Major Hart.

"Yes," said the Major, "what an awful mess. Wretched business all around."

"Very," said the Inspector. "She's a strange girl, your wife."

"Do you think—you don't think—that she was involved with the murder, do you?"

"I think she knows more than she's saying. It wasn't a little boy who killed that girl, that's for one thing. It's physically impossible. So I don't believe that part of the story at all. She could be covering up for some bloke."

"I think she's telling the truth," said the Major.

"But you don't really know her, do you?" asked the Inspector. "I've got the evidence I need to arrest her, you know. The button, and the lying, not to mention letting a crime go unreported. But I can't put her in jail on her wedding night, so I'll leave her be, if you promise me you'll keep your eye on her. I can look into her story of the young boy and see if anything turns up. Perhaps it will. I'll say good night to you, then, but I'm afraid I'll have to come round first thing in the morning and make the arrest." He opened the closet door and removed his coat from the hanger and shrugged himself into it.

Coral stood inside the library door and listened to the two men discuss her. Men are so stupid, she thought. They don't understand anything. It is unfair to be a woman in this world. She remembered the little girl in the woods. Taking turns, they had said, but of course that wasn't so. Of course they had not.

Someone—it had to have been Mrs Prence—had turned back the new silken coverlet on the huge canopied bed, exposing the pillows and sheets beneath it, and this revelation seemed almost indecent to Coral. It was cold in the room, and she could hear the rain beating the gravel of the front drive.

A long white nightgown, made of eyelet and lace, was carefully laid out across the foot of the bed, and beside it squatted her shabby little suitcase. Coral stared at the nightgown and for a moment thought it must be Mrs Prence's, left behind, and then realised it had been put there for her.

There was a soft knock on the door. "Come in," Coral called.

Mrs Prence opened the door and stood for a moment in the doorway, looking around the room as if she had never seen it before, or as if looking for some sort of damage or alteration Coral might have performed. Then she entered the room and closed the door behind her and leant back against it, either barring someone else from entering or Coral from escaping, or perhaps both. Something about Mrs Prence had been mysteriously altered, Coral thought. It was as if a film had been made and her character had been softened for the screen and a more attractive actress had been cast in her part. Or perhaps it was only the result of the golden shades on the bedside lamps, and the wine she and the Major had drunk with dinner.

"I just wanted to make sure you have everything you need for the night, ma'am," Mrs Prence said.

Coral said that she did.

Mrs Prence walked to the foot of the bed. "This belonged to Charlotte," she said. "Do you know about Charlotte?" Her voice had changed, too: unbarbed, caught low in her throat.

"The Major's sister?"

"Yes. Such a lovely girl. Poor Charlotte." Mrs Prence touched the nightgown delicately, as if there was still a body inside of it. "This was part of her trousseau. When she died, Mrs Hart kept it all and said, 'I shall make a gift of this to Clement's bride.' And then of course the war came and Major Hart was injured so wretched and Mrs Hart fell ill and the trousseau was forgotten in the attic but the other day I remembered and as it was Mrs Hart's wish up to the attic I go and there's the trunk and I open it up and right on top is this lovely gown for Charlotte's wedding night, and I when I packed your things for you to take to the Swan I saw your nightdress and I thought, Poor thing, she can't wear that tired old thing on her wedding night, so I take this one down from the attic and wash it in lavender and rosewater and iron it out, and here it is for you."

"Thank you Mrs Prence," said Coral. "It was very kind of you."

"Well, it's what Mrs Hart wanted. God rest her soul." She touched the embroidered bodice of the nightgown. "It was all handmade by nuns," she said. "Catholics. Virgins. In France. Or Spain, perhaps—I don't remember. But it's foreign, I know."

"It's beautiful," said Coral.

"I hope your talk with Inspector Hoke hasn't upset you," said Mrs Prence. "I think it's beastly of him, come sniffing about on your wedding day. It's a sacred day, I think, even if you were married by a magistrate. God still sees it, I'm sure."

"Yes," said Coral. "I'm sure he does."

Mrs Prence stepped back from the bed. She reached her hand into the pocket of her apron, pulled it out, and opened her fist to reveal a crush of pink petals. "The boy from the flower shop gave me these rose petals this afternoon. 'What am I to do with these?' I asked him. 'Sprinkle them on the wedding bed,' says he. 'It's a tradition.' Well, I've never heard of it—petals in the bed. Have you?"

"In books, I think," said Coral.

"In fairy tales, perhaps," said Mrs Prence. "Do you want them?" She held out her opened palm.

"No," said Coral.

"I thought not," said Mrs Prence. "It's why I didn't do what he said."

"Oh, give them to me," said Coral. "They can't hurt, can they?"

"Hurt?" said Mrs Prence.

"They won't do any harm," said Coral.

"Well, that's no reason to put them in your bed."

"I don't know what I'll do with them," said Coral, "but I'd like them, since he gave them to you."

Mrs Prence pressed the petals into Coral's open hand and then looked about the room. "The drapes!" she said. "I forgot to close them." She walked to the windows and heroically pulled the heavy drapes across both of them, as if she were shielding Coral from a scene of great devastation, or merely the audience of the great wet outdoors. Then she paused in the middle of the room and looked strangely at Coral.

"Is there anything—anything at all—that you would like to tell me?"

"Tell you?" asked Coral.

"Tell me, or say to me. Something that troubles you, that would be a relief to share."

"No," said Coral. "There is nothing."

"Because if there was, I would listen calmly and not judge you. I know I have not been a good friend to you, and I would like to change that now."

"That is very kind of you," said Coral, "and I appreciate your kindness, Mrs Prence. I welcome it, and hope to return it."

"Tell me, then! I know that you are troubled by something. You have no mother, no friend. Tell me what is troubling you, and I will share your burden."

"Nothing troubles me," said Coral. "There is no burden."

"You cannot fool me," said Mrs Prence. "I know that there is."

"I think you can leave now, Mrs Prence. Thank you for all you have done. And for your lovely gift. But please, I would like you to leave me alone now."

Mrs Prence said nothing. She stood there as if frozen, with an odd, struck expression upon her face.

"Good night," said Coral.

"Forgive me," said Mrs Prence. "I was only trying to be a friend to you. But I am rusty in the ways of friendship and perhaps said something wrong. Forgive me."

"There is nothing to forgive," said Coral. She walked to the door and opened it.

After a moment Mrs Prence roused herself and walked with dignity out of the room. Coral closed the door behind her, and was alone.


Coral sat on the bed for a while after Mrs Prence left. It was very quiet in the house; outside, the rain fell, but inside the house, nothing seemed to utter, or move, and Coral hoped that by sitting silently and stilly on the bed, she might not disturb the diorama she felt she was in, for she did not want anything else to happen to her ever again. She could not imagine anything that was not bad or disappointing happening. She thought of the stuffed hummingbirds, frozen within their glass dome. It would be better, she thought, to have your insides taken out and replaced with sawdust, and have tiny glass beads for eyes, and be imprisoned beneath a glass dome.

The Major was taking a bath; he had told Coral he would continue to use his own bathroom and she could use his mother's, which was en suite. She did not want him to find her dressed and sitting on the bed—she did not want him to find her at all, she realised—so she took the nightgown into the bathroom and ran a bath for herself. As the tub filled, the shadow of a body bloomed like a bruise along its surface—the result, no doubt, of many years of porcelain slowly abraded by flesh.

Coral undressed and tossed the petals into the steaming water. They unfurled and floated like tiny pink lily pads on the jittering surface. She watched them for a moment. Some gave up and sank slowly to the bottom of the tub, but many remained. She lowered her body gingerly into the hot rose-scented water.

*Bunny*, Mr DeVries had called her, *pink bunny, cotton-tailed bunny*. And other, filthy things. The children had a pet rabbit, a rather sad animal kept in a hutch outside the garage, with alarmingly large yellow teeth. She remembered how ugly Mr DeVries's penis had looked, jutting up from him, red and angry, like an already bloodied knife.

She got out of the bath and dried herself. She lowered the stiff linen tent of the nightgown over her naked body. *Skin a rabbit*, her mother had said when she was very young, which meant she must raise her arms above her head so that an article of clothing could be flensed. Gruesome, really.

She sat on the bed and waited. She felt her body chill beneath the thin layer of linen, which she realised had been pressed hard and stiff by Mrs Pearce: it was not a gift but a punishment. A hairshirt. After a moment she opened the drawer of the night table beside the bed and looked in at the jumble of crimped tubes and ancient bottles of lotions and unguents. Dirty bits of ribbons, and hankies, and nubs of pencils. A prescription bottle read: *Mrs Edith Hart, take 1 tablet every six hours or as needed for pain*. A wooden baby

Jesus crèche figurine, missing his left arm, was stuck to an un-
wrapped piece of toffee. Coral shuddered and closed the drawer.

Someone knocked on the door. The Major. Clement.

"Yes?" she called.

"It's me," he said. "May I come in?"

"Just a moment," she said. She felt panicked, almost dazed.

"Coral?" he called.

She sought refuge in the bathroom. "Come in!" she called, and
then shut the bathroom door.

She heard him enter the bedroom. He was quiet a moment
and then, almost plaintively, once again called her name, as if she
might have escaped out the window or simply disappeared.

"Yes," she said. "I'm in the bath. I'll be right out."

"Oh, darling!" he said. "Take your time. No rush."

She heard the relief in his voice, and a tenderness, too. She had
always considered herself a timid and sensitive girl, but suddenly,
in comparison to him, she felt brazen and unkind. She realised she
had been changed by the things that had recently happened to her,
changed into someone she felt was other than herself. She looked
at the mirror. Her throat was brilliantly flushed and a pink splotch,
like ineptly applied rouge, decorated each of her cheeks. Her forehead was damp and glistening. She looked like someone with a high
fever who had been recently throttled. She rinsed her face with cold
water and then patted it with a towel, but when she faced the mirror
again she looked exactly the same. She observed herself for a moment, as if some change might magically occur, but her reflection
was steadfast.

When Coral emerged from the bathroom, the Major was standing in the alcove by the windows, swaddled in a dressing gown,
contemplating his slippered feet.

She stood by the bed, and after a moment he looked up at her.
"Coral!" he cried. "How lovely you are!" He held out both his hands,
and although it was an instinctive gesture he could not help, it appeared to Coral as if he thought he was in a musical film and

expected her to skip across the room, take his hands, and sing. He was costumed for such a role, or perhaps for a historical drama: his brocade bathrobe was as heavy as a topcoat and edged at every seam with silk piping; its shoulders were padded; braided frogs fastened it snuggly across his broad chest; a tasselled cord, as thick as a child's wrist, was cinched at its waist, and its skirt fell almost to the floor, just above black velvet slippers that bore a golden crest on each vamp.

But she just stood there, looking at him, and after a moment he became aware of his awkwardly proffered hands and clasped them together. "There is something I must tell you," he said.

"Oh—" she said. "Yes. There is something I must tell you, too."

"It is about Hoke," he said rushingly, as if he had not heard what she had said. "He is coming back here in the morning. He says he has enough evidence to arrest you."

"The button?"

"The button—yes. And what you told him—that you had seen the girl, but said nothing."

"Is that a crime?"

"I don't know," he said. "All I know is that he will be back here in the morning and arrest you."

"And so?" she asked. She shivered and held herself tightly, trying to contain the chill.

"You're cold," he said. "Why don't you get into the bed? It will be warmer."

She looked at the golden coverlet drawn tightly across the flat expanse of the bed and neatly folded over at the top, exposing its voluptuous pillows, and it looked to her as if it were inviolable, uninhabitable. She shook her head. "No," she said.

He seemed to understand her mysterious inability to disturb the bed and said, "Well, here, then, take my robe." He unfastened the velvet frogs that held it closed along one side of this chest and then unloosed the cord that girded his waist, and shrugged himself out of the robe. He moved towards the bed, holding the robe by its padded shoulders. "Sit on the bed," he said. She did, and he draped the robe around her. It felt more heavy than warm, like a lead blanket.

He stood for a moment beside the bed, watching her, as if the robe might crush or flatten her, but after a moment he sat beside her. Beneath the robe he wore navy blue silk pyjamas in the Cossack style; he looked quite handsome in them, if a bit absurd, like a character in a pantomime. She had the notion that they were bought especially for this night, and the idea of him shopping for them—for surely he had done it alone—caused an almost overwhelming tenderness to well in her, an involuntary response to the decency and gentleness of him. She almost reached out and touched him.

"What should I do?" she asked.

"May I ask you a question?"

"Yes," she said. "Of course."

"Did you—did you have anything to do with that girl in the woods?"

"No," she said. "Nothing. Except for seeing her there that day. But nothing else."

"So you did see her?"

"Yes," she said. "As I told the Inspector."

"Then why, for God's sake, did you say nothing to anyone?"

She pulled his robe tighter around her. "I don't know," she said. "It was almost like a dream; I wasn't absolutely sure I'd seen it, and I was so confused . . ."

"About what?"

"Everything!" she said. "About my life, and what you had asked me—and everything. And it disturbed me—"

"Then you should have told someone."

"Yes," she said. "I know. But I didn't. I didn't know how, or to whom, I should speak. And it went away, like a dream . . ."

"But it wasn't a dream," he said. "It's come back."

"I know," she said.

"I think you must leave here," he said. "Now, tonight. It is the only thing I can think for you to do."

"And what shall I do?" she asked. "Where shall I go?"

"To London, I suppose. You said you had a friend there."

"No, not a friend . . ."

"But someone you know. Someone you could stay with, surely, until . . ."

"Until what? When?"

"I don't know. Perhaps they will find the boy you saw, or perhaps it was someone else, and they will find him. God only knows what will happen. So you must stay away until it does." He paused for a moment and then said, "It would be best, I think, if I do not know where you are."

Coral stood up from the bed and removed the robe. "Yes," she said, "I suppose it would be best for you."

"For us both, I think. That way I can be perfectly honest with Hoke."

"Yes," she said.

"I will give you money, of course."

Coral said nothing.

"You can stay here if you would like. If you did nothing, and think your innocence can be proved, it is really up to you. You are welcome to stay here, if you are prepared for the consequences."

Coral looked at him. "Is it a great relief to you?"

"What?"

"That I must go like this?"

"Coral! You misunderstand me. I am only trying to help you, protect you. I only just said you may stay here. My heart is broken, I thought we would begin a new life together—I love you!"

"I'm sorry," she said. "I don't know what to think."

"It is because I am worried for you that I think you must leave. I want to protect you."

"So you must banish me."

"No. Can't we— What do you want? My darling, what do you want? Do you want to stay here and face Hoke tomorrow?"

"No."

"Well, then, what do you want?"

"What do I want? It is not really a question of that. I agree with you—it is best for me to go away now, tonight. All of this has been a mistake."

"You think that?"

"Yes," she said. "Don't you? Especially now?"

"No," he said. "When this horrible business is finished, I can be in touch with you, and you can come back here. If you want to come back here. Perhaps you will not. Perhaps it is you who are relieved."

Coral said nothing.

"Are you relieved?"

"No," said Coral. "How can I know? How can I know anything at a moment like this?"

He looked at her for a moment. "Forgive me," he said. "I thought you might know that."

The Major telephoned the Loftings and asked if Coral could stay the night with them, and could they drive her to the station in Leicester for the first London train in the morning? She could, and they would. They would drive round to fetch her right away.

The Major left her to dress and gather her things, as if she had many, or really any, for that matter. Her small suitcase, which had followed her to The Black Swan and back, had yet to be unpacked, and so stood ready for another journey. There was one thing she wanted, though: the sapphire ring. She would have liked to leave it behind her, forget it and the episode it represented, but she could not afford to, for it was the most valuable thing she owned, and it could always be pawned. She had secreted it in her little bedroom when she had arrived at Hart House, for she did not like to see it or keep it in her possession. She climbed the stairs to the third floor of the house and entered the little room that had briefly been hers. It was just as she had found it the night she arrived at Hart House, bare and unwelcoming, completely devoid of any warmth or colour or charm. She reached up and took the mirror off its hook on the wall and laid it facedown upon the bed. Her ring was still there, hanging from the wire that stretched across the mirror's back. She untwisted one end of the wire and unthreaded the ring. How much was it worth? Perhaps not very much, but it was a real gemstone and real gold, so it must be worth something.

She hung the mirror back on the wall and sat for a moment on the bed, the thin mattress creaking the bedsprings. She put the ring on her ring finger.


The Major was waiting for her in the front hall when she descended the stairs with her suitcase and medical bag.

"They should be here any minute," he said. "But come, sit with me in the drawing room."

Of course, he did not want to sit with her in the library, because that is where their relationship, such as it was, had bloomed, and to spend their final moments together there would be excruciating. So they went and sat in the large, dark, cold drawing room, she on the settee and he on one of the spindly-legged chairs. He turned on a lamp but did not switch on the electrical fire. For a moment they said nothing, and then he said, "Oh, Coral, I don't know what to say."

"I know," she said. "Neither do I."

"I do think it's best you go away now, but it's so awful. It's such damned bad luck, isn't it?"

"Yes," she said.

"Listen," he said, "they should be here at any moment, but I wanted to give you this." He held an envelope out to her.

"No," she said. "I don't need it."

"Of course you do," he said. "Please take it. I can't let you leave without it. Please. If you don't need it, you can always return it. But please take it."

She took the envelope of money.

"When you are settled, you must write to Dolly and Robin and let them know how to contact you, and I can send you more. But don't write to me—who knows what Hoke will do when he discovers you've bolted. And that way, when the coast is clear, I'll know where to find you. Will you do that, Coral?"

"Yes," she said.

They heard the crunch of gravel in the drive.

"Ah," he said, "they're here."

"Yes," she said. She stood up. She looked around the room, as if there might be something of hers to collect, as if she were about to leave a house she had authentically lived in. But of course there was nothing. There was nothing of anybody's; it was that kind of house: the people who lived in it made no real impression upon it. But then she remembered the stash of excreta she had found in the bedside drawer upstairs, and realised that all these things were hidden beneath the pristine, impersonal surfaces of the house.

The Major stood as well. He wore a stricken look upon his face, and he, too, looked wildly around the room, but nothing in the room could help or save them. "Oh, Coral," he said. "May I embrace you?"

She did not answer—it would have been too awful to answer him—but moved towards him and into his suddenly open arms and pressed her face against his chest. He still wore only his pyjamas and she could feel the warmth of his flesh and the beating of his heart through their thin silken skin. Instinctively she raised her face and found his falling towards her, and suddenly their mouths and lips frantically answered one another's. Then the bell chimed and they heard Dolly's voice, and they pulled themselves apart.

# PART THREE

Soon after Coral arrived in London, she found a woman who put an end to her pregnancy.

She wrote to Clement, in care of the Loftings, but heard nothing back. She wrote to him again a few weeks later, when she moved into a new room in a large house on Grantley Terrace, and regularly returned to the place she had originally stayed, to enquire for mail. But there was none, and her second letter, which had included her new address, also went unanswered. She wrote a third, and final, letter.

She was hired by the National Health as a visiting nurse, and it suited her well. It was good to see her patients in their homes, change their bandages, give them injections, bathe them, change their linen, even empty their bedpans, and then leave at the end of every day—leave and return alone to her little room with the bed and dresser and chair and gas ring and the trees outside the window and the sound of the piano coming up from downstairs. Madame Paszkowska, her landlady, was a pianist, and often played. Apparently she had been quite well-known on the continent before the war.

Initially, Coral was shocked that she did not hear from Clement, but then it made perfect sense to her: of course she did not hear from him. She never would. Dolly had certainly told him about the baby, and that, combined with the awful business with the girl in the wood, had caused him to be done with her. Perhaps he had sincerely meant to reconnect with her when he sent her away, but once she was gone, and it was over, he must have realised what a mistake it all had been. It had all been a mistake. It was over.

It was more difficult to banish Inspector Hoke from her mind. For a while she thought she saw him everywhere she went, and was sure he would be waiting for her every evening when she returned to Grantley Terrace. But then, slowly, she realised he was not going to appear, that if he had meant to find her he would have done so already—she had made no attempt to hide herself—and she understood that that burden, that shadow, was, like the baby, gone.

Coral thought: This is more happiness than I deserve, even if it is not exactly happiness. But it was a sort of freedom: there had been so many problems—it had all been problems, everything had been a problem for such a long time—and to be released from that perpetually increasing darkness was a kind of joy.


There was only one other tenant living in the house on Grantley Terrace with Madame Paszkowska: an elderly woman called Miss Lingle. She lived in a suite of rooms on the floor below Coral with her pet rabbit, Pansy, who sat all day upon Miss Lingle's lap. Although she left her door open and smiled at Coral when she passed by every morning and evening, she never spoke to Coral, and Coral did not speak to Miss Lingle. Once or twice Pansy managed to escape Miss Lingle's clutch and hop up the stairs, where Coral would find her waiting, as she was apparently either unable or disinclined to hop back down the stairs, no matter how persistently Coral encouraged her. On these occasions, Coral would carry the rabbit, who was surprisingly heavy, down the stairs to Miss Lingle, who seemed unconcerned by Pansy's abandonment and accepted her return as if Coral had simply borrowed her for a spell.

A similar cordial distance existed between Coral and Madame Paszkowska: with the exception of polite greetings they spoke only about matters concerning the house and Coral's residency therein.

Madame Paszkowska's daughter, Irene, lived elsewhere with her husband, a darkly silent man named David Chaiken who published books about paintings, but used her mother's drawing room to give piano lessons on many evenings and weekend afternoons. She, too, was pleasant yet distant with Coral, if their paths happened to cross, and the resulting privacy and solitude suited Coral, as her nursing brought her every day into confining spaces often oversaturated with life and in contact with lonely patients as needful of companionship as care.

There was a room on the second floor, beside Madame Paszkowska's room, that was apparently uninhabited, for its door was never opened. One morning a few days before Christmas—it would be the first Christmas Coral passed in London, the Christmas after the Christmas she had nursed the DeVries children— Coral paused on the second-floor landing on her way downstairs because the door was open. She moved closer and peered inside. The room was small and dark; the walls were painted a deep olive-gold and the tall golden drapes where closed against the morning light. The room contained a bed, a cupboard, and a desk piled high with paper and books. Madame Paszkowska was folding clean sheets onto the mattress. She sensed Coral's presence in the doorway and looked up at her.

"Good morning, Miss Glynn," she said.

Coral said good morning.

"Lazlo is coming," said Madame Paszkowska. "My son. Did you know that I had a son as well as a daughter?"

"No," said Coral.

"He will be here today, to spend the Christmas with me. He will be here tonight. All the way from Lowestoft, he comes. He manages a hotel there. But he has holiday for Christmas."

"How nice for you," said Coral.

"Tonight we have a little party, Irene will come with her David and my friend Mrs Sturtevant from number twelve. You will join us, please? To greet my son and welcome the holiday?"

"Oh," said Coral, "thank you, it's very kind, but I'm sure you would rather be with your family and friend. I don't want to intrude."

"You do not intrude. You intrude if you do not come. Miss Lingle will come. We have some music and drink schnapps. Today I make *pierniczki* and *rogaliki*. Delicious cookies."

"Thank you," said Coral. "I will be very happy to come."

"Good," said Madame Paszkowska.


On her way home that evening, Coral stopped at Shreve & Sons and bought a decorated tin filled with crystallised ginger and orange peel. They wrapped it for her in silver paper tied with a red ribbon and Coral thought she had done right, that it was an appropriate gift, and felt adult as she descended the stairs later that evening. Someone was playing the piano in the drawing room, a piece her brother had played. Chopin, she thought. She paused on the stairs and listened, and thought of James. Although she had loved her parents, they did not return to her thoughts as often as James did. He came to her, unbidden, at the slightest provocation: the boy in the flower shop; a boy on the street; a dark green Raleigh bicycle leaning against a building; some notes of music; espadrilles, which James had brought back from his school trip to France and wore until they fell to pieces—all these things caught James up with her.

Coral waited until the piece was finished and then entered the drawing room. Mrs Sturtevant and Miss Lingle were seated on the sofa; David was sitting in a chair and Irene perched on the pouf beside him; Madame Paszkowska was seated at the piano; and a very tall young man with a wonderful shock of golden blond hair stood in front of the fireplace, one long arm laid along the mantel, smiling at her. He was very handsome, almost beautiful, although his beauty was slightly obscured by the suit he was wearing, which had obviously been tailored to fit a larger, shorter man, for it hung too wide across his chest and hips and too short at his wrists and ankles. Despite these flaws, he wore it confidently, as if he knew that a suit that fit him well would make him excruciatingly beautiful.

Madame Paszkowska stood up from the piano and approached Coral, who held her silver-wrapped present before her ceremonially, with both hands, as if she had come a very long way to present it to Madame Paszkowska.

"Miss Glynn!" Madame Paszkowska exclaimed. "How very kind of you." She took the gift from Coral and handed it to Irene, who had also stood up. "Here is my son, Lazlo Paszkowski," she said, indicating the young man, who had detached himself from the fireplace and stepped forwards to greet Coral.

Coral said hello to him and shook his hand and then greeted the other guests, all of whom she knew.

"Your dress—so beautiful!" said Irene.

"Yes," said Miss Lingle. "How pretty you look in it." She smiled kindly at Coral, as it was she who had fastened the clasps on the back of the dress, and therefore felt partially responsible for the dramatic effect it made. Coral blushed. She had not worn the dress since her wedding, although she sometimes took it out of the wardrobe and contemplated it. If you looked carefully, you could see where Mrs Henderson had mended the seam, the slightly irregular stitches binding the torn fabric back together. But only if you knew where to look.

She sat on the sofa between the two older ladies. Lazlo handed her a little crystal glass of schnapps, and filled everyone else's glasses, and made a toast to his mother, his sister, and all the other beautiful women present. Coral sipped the schnapps as Irene played the piano, and then Madame Paszkowska played again, accompanying Miss Lingle while she sang, in her surprisingly steady and strong soprano voice, several carols and folk songs, finishing with the barcarole from *The Tales of Hoffmann*.

And it was then revealed that Rosamund Lingle had been a very famous singer early in the century, and had sung at Covent

Garden. Coral had been aware of Madame Paszkowska's successful career as a classical pianist, for there hung, on the wall alongside the staircase, a series of framed programs and photographs
illustrating this fact, but she had never suspected that Miss Lingle, who seemed quite simple and sat all day stroking her pet
rabbit, had also been a person of noted accomplishment. And this
revelation caused Coral to feel ashamed and downcast, for she
had felt smugly superior to the old lady every morning as she hastened past her door in her nurse's uniform, hurrying out to be engaged, somewhat heroically, she imagined Miss Lingle imagined,
with the world. How was it ever possible to know who, or what,
people really were? They were all like coins, with two sides, or dice,
with six.

When Miss Lingle's program was complete, Madame Paszkowska asked Coral if she would like to sing or play, as if to do so
was a talent bestowed upon every inhabitant of that house. Coral
admitted that she had no talent for either, and so could contribute
nothing to the evening.

"Nonsense, Miss Glynn," Lazlo said. "You contribute your beauty,
and who can say what that is worth?"

Coral was about to answer that beauty could not compare to
talent, but she realised that saying this implied that she considered
herself beautiful, however inferior beauty was to talent. She blushed
and said that she wished she had a talent.

Lazlo said her blushing made her more beautiful than ever.

Coral was aware that he was flirting with her; she had been
aware of him watching her ever since she had entered the room,
and she thought perhaps she should not have worn her wedding
dress, for surely it was the dress that accounted for any beauty she
had, and it seemed immodest to wear it if that was true. One should
look presentable, of course, but to try to look beautiful, which effort
implied a belief that one could achieve beauty, made her feel uneasy,
for she felt that courting the attention of men could only lead to
disaster. And so, in an effort to divert Lazlo's attention from her-

self, she said that her brother could play the piano, and had in fact often played the piece that Madame Paszkowska had been playing before she joined the party; was it Chopin?

"It was Liszt," said Madame Paszkowska, "but Liszt and Chopin sound much alike to the untrained ear."

"And sometimes even to the ear that is trained," Irene kindly added.

"Is your brother in London?" asked Madame Paszkowska. "I wish I had known; he could have joined us this evening."

Coral was about to say that her brother no longer lived anywhere, when she realised that there was really no need to share this information. Perhaps it was the two glasses of schnapps she had drunk, but her lack of any family always made her seem somewhat pathetic, as if their complete disappearance reflected poorly on her. She might as well have a living brother.

"No," she said, "he doesn't live in London. He lives in Harrington."

"Is he older than you or younger than you?" Miss Lingle asked.

"We are the same age," Coral decided. "We are twins."

"I can't imagine what it is like to have a twin," said Lazlo. "It was torture enough having a sister. I suppose it is because I am so vain. The very idea of anyone so similar to me is most disturbing."

"Well, being brother and sister, we are not identical," said Coral. "We are fraternal twins."

"Harrington—is that where you are from?" asked David.

"No," said Coral. "I am from Huddlesford."

"And what does your brother do in Harrington?" asked Madame Paszkowska.

"He manages a florist's shop," said Coral. "He is very good with flowers. That is a kind of talent, I think. Another one that I do not have." She laughed, and then she stopped abruptly, for she felt she had gone too far. It was the schnapps.

•

Coral woke later that night from a very deep sleep. Someone, she felt, had just opened the door and stepped into her room. Had she been dreaming? She lay very still in bed and listened and tried make sense of the darkness around her. She heard someone breathing and felt an especial stillness near to the bed, the bottled energy of a body trying not to move. "Hello?" she said.

"It's me, Lazlo." He did not move.

"Lazlo!" She reached out and turned on the lamp that sat on the bedside table, and there he was, standing in the centre of the room, wearing only his trousers and a sleeveless undershirt, in his stocking feet. He stepped closer and leant towards her, and she thought he was going to touch her, and she almost screamed, but he was reaching only for the lamp, which he turned off. The nearness of him had released a scent of something: man, smoke. It was briefly pungent in the dark.

"Good night, Mr Light," he said.

He was drunk. She had drunk several little glasses of the silvery schnapps and felt tipsy when she went to bed, but the shock of him entering her room had cleared her head. She turned the light back on.

"Get out," she said. "Get out or I'll scream."

"No," he said. "Oh, Coral! Don't be frightened. I can't sleep. I only want to talk to you. Please. In the dark."

"No," said Coral. "It isn't proper. You can't enter someone's private room in the middle of the night . . ."

"I'll sit over there," he said, pointing to the chair in the corner of the room. "Just for a moment or two. Please. Just sit in the dark and talk for a moment. Wouldn't that be nice?"

"No," said Coral. "Go back to your room or I shall scream."

He sat down in the chair and began to weep. He covered his face with his hands.

Coral watched him, saying nothing. Was he really weeping, or only pretending?

"Please shut out the light," he said. "I'm ashamed to be seen weeping." He removed his hands and looked at her. "I mean no trouble. Please."

Coral turned out the light but continued to sit upright in bed. After a moment he seemed to stop weeping. It was quiet. If she didn't know he was sitting on the chair in the corner of her room, she would not know he was there.

Then he spoke again. "Would you mind if I smoke a cigarette?" he asked.

"No," said Coral.

"Would you like one as well?"

"No," said Coral.

She heard him rummage in his trouser pockets and then he flicked on a lighter and dipped his head, with a cigarette already in his mouth, into the flame. He snapped the lighter shut and the cigarette brightened as he inhaled.

"You're not still scared, are you?" he asked.

"Yes," said Coral. "Of course I am. And tired. I wish you would leave."

"If you're tired, you aren't scared," he said. "You can't be both."

"I can," she said.

"Then you are very special," he said. "But I knew that—that you were special—from the moment you appeared downstairs. So beautiful, so special."

"You're talking rubbish," said Coral. "You're drunk. You should go to bed."

"Truth is what the drunken speak, not rubbish," he said. "Everyone knows that. Truth."

Coral said nothing.

"Have you got a man?" he asked.

"No," said Coral.

"It isn't right, a beautiful girl like you, all alone. My mother says you're lonesome as a nun."

More, thought Coral: Nuns have Jesus to love, to go on and on about. I have no one.

"I think you need a man," Lazlo said. "It is a feeling I have. It kept me from sleeping."

Coral said nothing. She could feel her drunken drowsiness returning, crawling out from where it had hidden at the shock of him.

"It would be a shame," he said, "for you to be alone, now that I am here. I don't think it's natural."

She did not speak because she wanted him to continue talking. Through the darkness she could now make out the pale glow of his naked arms and his face, which appeared each time he raised the cigarette to his lips.

"Christ, but it's cold in here," he said. "There's no heat at all. And me sitting here half-naked, freezing to death. Christ."

"So go to bed," she said. "Go to bed if you are cold. You'll soon be warm."

"No," he said. "My bed's like ice. You couldn't know how cold it is." He stood up, and she watched him stub his cigarette on the window ledge. He moved aside the curtain and looked out the window. The gentle light from outside fell upon his face. "It's snowing outside," he said. "Did you know that it's snowing?"

"No," said Coral.

He was suddenly standing beside the bed, looking down at her. Perhaps she had fallen asleep for a moment, for she did not remember him moving from the window to the bedside. She looked up at him.

"How beautiful you are," he said. "And it's snowing. You don't want me to freeze to my death, do you? A man could freeze in weather like this."

She shook her head, and heard it rasp against the pillowcase. She reached up a hand and held it so that it obscured his face, and then moved it aside, revealing him again. He reached up with both hands and pulled his braces off of his shoulders and let them fall to his sides. One fell faster than the other so they made two separate little smacks against his trouser legs. And then he peeled his undershirt off over his head. "Look at me now," he said, "shivering to death, and you as warm as you can be. It isn't fair." He unbuttoned his flies and stepped carefully out of his trousers, and then scooped his under-pants down his long legs, revealing his cock, which appeared to be slowly reinventing itself. "Ah, look at him," he said. "How brave he is. Despite the cold, he is the only part of me that is warm."

Coral said nothing.

Lazlo's cock got bigger, and lifted up away from him, like a baby reaching out its tiny arm.

"Touch him," he said.

Coral touched him, just barely clasping the tube of flesh, and it was warm. It twitched in her hand and she let it go. "You aren't cold," she said.

"I am," said Lazlo. "Feel here." He reached out and took her hand and placed it against his thigh, held it against the curve of his leg.

"It's warm," she said. "You're warm."

"No," said Lazlo. "Feel this." He reached down and laid his hand against her cheek. It was freezing. She took her hand from his leg and held it against his hand against her cheek until it felt warm. He slowly withdrew his hand and moved it down her neck, his fin-gers touching her throat, and she turned her face aside as he slid it beneath her nightgown and touched her breast. He stood like that, his hand on her skin, and she felt her breast swell within his loose grasp, as if rising up to meet him, and she heard him mumble something—it sounded like "Yes, yes"—and she closed her eyes and shifted over in the bed, towards the wall, making a space be-side her.

He came to her room every night of the week he stayed in Lon-don, came at some point after everyone had gone to bed and left each morning before dawn. During the day or evening, if he hap-pened to encounter her, he treated her with the same cordiality as his mother, as if the night was another country that had severed all diplomatic relations with the day.

When she returned to Grantley Terrace on the evening of the last day of the year, and climbed the stairs to her room, she noticed that the door to Lazlo's little bedroom was open, and the mattress lay bare upon the bed, and all of his clothes, which had been strewn about the room all week, were gone. The window was open wide, to air out the funk of his smoke. Lazlo was gone, gone back to Lowestoft, gone without a word.

One day, after she had been in London for over a year, Madame Paszkowska stopped Coral in the front hallway as she returned from work and told her that her room would be painted the following day, and it would be a help if she would remove everything from the walls and window ledge.

There was only one painting in the room, which had been there when Coral arrived, left behind by some former tenant, as most of the objects in her room seemed to have been, for it was obvious there was no singular, unifying aesthetic connecting any one piece to another: they were all castoffs. People had hurriedly left this room countless times, for as many reasons, gathering up the things they could carry with them and leaving the rest behind, and it was the detritus of all these lives that furnished Coral's room. And she did not mind it: there was something rich and welcoming about the motley collection of things; they augmented the meagreness of her own existence, for she did not have enough possessions to fill even a room.

When she lowered the painting—two robins standing on the rim of a nest in the crotch of a tree, observing the five blue eggs that lay potently within it—she was surprised to see Mrs DeVries's sapphire ring hanging from the picture wire. She had hidden it there when she first arrived at Grantley Terrace, keeping it safe until the time she would need to pawn it, which she was sure would be soon. But things had worked out far better and more quickly than she had expected, and the money that Major Hart had given to her had lasted until she had found her new job.

The woman in the pawnshop on Bethnal Green Road suffered a toothache and had a bandage tied around her head and jaw. She placed a rather grubby velvet pad on the wooden counter and motioned for Coral to deposit the ring upon it. Then she turned on a lamp and stuck a jeweller's loupe in her eye and examined the ring.

"It's gold," said Coral. "I know it is. And the stone is real. It's a sapphire."

"It's flawed," said the woman.

"Flawed?" asked Coral.

"Occlusions," said the woman. "And the gold is very worn. The shaft is weak."

Coral said nothing.

The woman placed the ring back upon the velvet pad and then removed the loupe from her eye. She turned off the lamp and named a price that seemed very low to Coral.

"I think it's worth more than that," said Coral. "Surely it is."

"Perhaps it is and perhaps it isn't," said the woman. "In any case, that is what I can give you for it. It's a fair price."

"It isn't enough," said Coral. "I want more."

"We all want more," said the woman, "but few of us get it."

Coral picked up the ring. "I shall keep it, then," she said. "It was my grandmother's."

"Yes, keep it," said the woman. "But come back when you need to sell it."

Her repossession of the ring awoke in Coral a strange compulsion, and on the following Saturday she took a train from Waterloo to Guildford, where she arrived late in the morning. It was an unusually warm spring day. She removed the jacket she was wearing over a sleeveless dress and felt the sun on her arms and face. It was a new dress, her best dress, navy blue with white polka dots, and she had bought navy blue shoes to go with it. Her bag was black, but perhaps with the dress and shoes it looked navy blue.

She walked up the street into town and had lunch at a café. She found that she was very hungry: she had eaten nothing that morning before leaving London. She had a cup of tea and egg on toast, and sat in the café, watching out the window at the people passing by along the High Street in the warm sunlight, everyone happy, for it was Saturday, and sunny, and they were shopping.

When she was finished with her lunch she stepped into the street. She looked back through the café window at her table, which had not yet been cleared, and the remnants of her meal remained there as blatant as evidence: she was a person in the world. She existed, and she was free.

She went into a draper's shop and bought an Irish linen tea towel and a porcelain eggcup. She bought these things not because she needed them, or even wanted them, but because she could. She asked if they would hold her items in the store so that she could return for them later. Of course, they would be happy to.

When she left the shop she walked purposefully along the street to the edge of the commercial district and turned onto Winchester Road. She remembered the way perfectly, even though it had been winter when she had been here before and now everything had a different feeling to it: the trees were leafy green and the gardens were full of flowers and the windows of the houses were open and the sun was hot on the street. At the end of Winchester Road she turned left onto Winslow Road. It was good that she remembered the number—41—because all the houses on the street looked the same to her. She stood for a moment across the street from number 41. The façade was covered in ivy, which she did not remember, nor did she remember that the door was painted blue. The windows were all shut and it seemed unnaturally still and quiet, even for a house. It did not appear as if anyone was home. She stood and waited, although she did not know for what. A man and young boy came out of the house she was standing in front of and stopped beside her. The man was holding the boy's hand; the boy wore spectacles and had a patch over one eye.

"Good afternoon," the man said.

"Good afternoon," said Coral. And then she said it again, to the boy, but he did not answer her. Perhaps he was deaf; there was an odd vacancy about him.

"Do you need help with something?" asked the man.

She realised she has been standing there for quite some time and looked suspicious. "Oh, no," she said. "Thank you, but no. I just—could you tell me, is that house—is that where the DeVrieses live?" She pointed at the house across the street.

"Oh, no," he said. "Not anymore. They've moved around the corner. Onto Lambkin Crescent. Number three, I believe."

"Oh," she said. "Thank you. Thank you very much."

"It's just up the hill on your left," the man said. "It's the brick house painted white."

"Thank you," Coral said again.

"Come along, Dickie," the man said, and he and the boy continued along the street.

Coral went the opposite way and turned onto Lambkin Crescent. Number 3 was indeed a brick house painted white. Before she could think and perhaps stop herself, she walked up the cement pathway and rang the bell.

Nothing happened.

She rang it again, and once again failed to elicit any response. It was quiet, and in the quiet she heard music, orchestral music, floating around the house from the back garden. She listened for a moment to make sure she had heard correctly, and as she listened a dog came around the corner of the house and sat down abruptly to scratch itself. Then it looked up at her.

"Hello," she said.

The dog cocked its head and continued to regard her with an uncanine neutrality. She remembered the yellow-toothed, desperate rabbits in the hutch at the bottom of the garden and supposed the

DeVrieses had moved onto dogs. There had been a cat, too, and kittens, she remembered.

After a moment the dog got up and disappeared back around the corner of the house. Her presence at the front door obviously did not interest him one way or another. Coral followed him. There was a paved yard on the side of the house with a gate leading into both the front and back garden; both gates were open. She stood in the yard and watched the dog cross the lawn and approach a man sitting low to the ground on a canvas sling-back chair that was facing away from her, reading a book that he held upon his lap. The music came from an old windup gramophone that sat upon a wooden chair that stood beside him. She remembered that he was keen about music. He was a music publisher, whatever that was. The dog whined and the man in the chair said, without looking up from his book, "What is it, Toby?"

She suddenly remembered that his Christian name was Walter, although she had of course never called him by that name. The children had called him Papa and Mrs DeVries had called him Terry. He was wearing a sleeveless vest and short pants. His white legs were crossed, one knee over the other; one of his large bare feet dangled in the sunlight. He had a glass of something—whiskey, probably—from which he occasionally sipped, on the grass beside his chair. Once or twice he reached out to stroke the dog, who seemed to only tolerate this attention.

For a moment she thought perhaps it was enough to have come this far, to have merely seen him. Because she did not know exactly why she had come, or what she exactly wanted, it was difficult to know what to do or when to leave.

It occurred to her that if she had a gun, she could kill him. Shoot him and walk calmly back to the station and return to London and no one would ever know. While she was thinking this, the dog whined again and Mr DeVries looked up from his book and saw her. He shielded his eyes with his hand. "Hello," he called. "Are you looking for Rosalind?"

She did not answer him.

"Hello," he said again, and got up from his chair. He laid his book splayed open upon the grass and walked towards her. He was smiling. His bare legs were very white, and hairy. He wore a sort of kerchief knotted around his neck. He looked more than a little ridiculous.

"Hello," he said again as he approached the gate into the side yard.

"Hello," she said then.

"Looking for Rosalind? I'm afraid she's not here." He drew closer but still did not recognise her. He was smiling. "She's on holiday with the kiddies," he said.

"I'm not here to see Rosalind," Coral said.

"Oh. Are you collecting for something? I'm afraid I haven't got any money on me at the moment."

"No," she said, "I'm not collecting."

"Oh," he said again. He sounded perplexed. "What is it, then? Can I help you with something?"

"Perhaps," said Coral.

"Look, who are you? What's this about?"

"Do you really not recognise me?" Coral asked.

"I don't," he said. "Who are you? Do I know you?"

"You did," said Coral.

He stepped a bit closer to her, but there was still a hedge and the fence between them. His face had changed: all the bonhomie had left it and was replaced by tension. "Look," he said, "what are you doing here? What do you want?"

"So you do remember me," said Coral.

"You've changed," he said.

"I suppose I have," said Coral. "A lot has happened to me."

He said nothing. After a moment, when she did not speak, he said, "What do you want?"

"Nothing," she said. "Nothing from you. I've come to give you something. Something I don't want."

"What?" he asked.

"This," she said. She twisted the ring off her finger and held it out to him.

He did not move. "What's that?" he asked.

"The ring," she said. "It belongs to your wife. I don't want it."

"Well, neither do I," he said. "And neither does she. Keep it."

"I told you, I don't want it. Take it."

"You came here to give me the ring back?" he asked.

"Yes," she said.

"That's odd," he said.

"I don't think it is," said Coral.

He walked towards her then and stood just beside the hedge, and reached out over it, over the fence, and took the ring from her. Their fingers did not touch; he was careful to touch only the ring. He held the ring in his palm and looked at it for a moment. And then he looked up at Coral. "I'm sorry," he said. "I'm very sorry for what happened to you. For what I did to you."

Coral said nothing.

"It was awful what I did to you," he said. "I'm sorry. Rosalind was in a depression because of the kids, and—" he paused. "No," he said. "There's no excuse. I'm sorry."

"There was a child," she said, "but it is gone. I had an abortion."

He winced then, and raised his hand with the ring up to cover his eyes and the ring fell in the grass at his feet.

"What can I do for you?" he asked. "Do you need money?"

"No," she said. "You can do nothing for me." She looked at him again for a moment and then, surprising herself, said, "Goodbye."

She turned and walked back around to the front of the house and then down the pathway and onto the street. Quickly she walked up to the corner and turned onto Winslow Road. The little boy with the glasses and the eye patch stood on the sidewalk in front of the house opposite number 41, as if he were waiting for her. He had a little stuffed monkey on a leash that he could somehow make jump up and down and clash little tin cymbals, and for his sake she pretended to be frightened and shrieked and jumped back, and the boy laughed, and she continued walking back to the High Street and she passed the café where she had eaten her lunch and then the shop were she had made her purchases—where the tea towel and eggcup waited behind the counter for her to collect—but she re- alised she did not want them anymore; perhaps she had not wanted them to begin with. Who knew what one wanted and what one didn't want?

# PART FOUR

The Loftings had separate bedrooms, and each was a kingdom unto itself. Dolly's boudoir has been described, but Robin's has not. It was a large, spare room, located at the far end of the hall from Dolly's, with windows on three sides, which made it the brightest room in the house as well as the coldest. The bare walls were painted a tea-stained cream, and the few pieces of furniture stood at a distance from one another, like unsociable guests at a cocktail party. Only a few personal effects were visible: a stuffed bear sat atop the bureau and a model plane hung by a nylon thread from the ceiling; a second thread had been severed, causing the plane to seem to be in a perpetual crashing nosedive towards the linoleum floor. Anyone seeing this room would assume it belonged to a boy—perhaps a dead boy, and that it had been left untouched in memory.

Every now and then Dolly would visit Robin's room while he was away and carefully search it, looking for she knew not what. She had no moral qualms about this inspection, for she reasoned that if they shared a bedroom, as so many married couples did, she would be privy to everything it contained, and therefore she had license to examine the contents of her husband's private chamber.

And though she often searched his spartan room, she never found anything that was hidden, nothing secret or thrilling. And this made her sad, for she would have liked to know that Robin had some sort of a secret life, for it is a burden to complement one's partner's life completely.

And then one day in the late spring, she found the letters,

hidden between *Stalky & Co.* and *The Light That Failed*, two of the
uniform editions of Kipling that Robin kept on his little bookshelf.
The envelopes were plain and addressed simply to C. Hart c/o
Lofting, Eustacia Villa, Harrington, Leicestershire. All three envelopes remained sealed. She immediately opened and read them.

*Dear Clement,*

   *I am here in London and have found a place to stay,*
*a hotel with weekly rates. The address to write to me is The*
*Pavilion Hotel, 24 Chiswick Street, London. I hope you are*
*well and that I hear from you soon. I am so sorry about the*
*trouble I have caused you by being foolish about the girl in*
*the woods. You have been so kind to me and I miss your*
*kindness. So please write to me here as soon as you are able.*

   *Truly yours,*
      *Coral*

*Dear Clement,*

   *I have moved from the Pavilion Hotel into a room in a*
*house on Grantley Terrace owned by a Polish woman. She is*
*very nice and the room is fine and I have a job now with the*
*National Health. So all is well with me. I've returned several*
*times to the Pavilion but there is no letter from you. I*
*suppose this means you have changed your feelings about me*
*and do not care to be in touch with me any longer. But*
*perhaps you did not receive my first letter? If that is the case*
*the address you can write to me now is Coral Glynn, c/o*
*Madame Wiola Paszkowska, 16 Grantley Terrace, London,*
*or you can write to the Pavilion Hotel, I will still check there*
*for mail, and they know me there and will keep it for me*
*(if you send something). I hope you are well and nothing*
*unfortunate has happened. Please write to me I miss you and*
*often think of you.*

      *Coral*

*Dear Clement,*

*It has been more than two months and I have not heard from you so I will not write to you again. I understand now why you sent me away and agree that is better this way, I am sorry I did not understand it then and bothered you with my letters. It was all a mistake and I am very sorry for whatever I have done but I know it is for the best. If you feel differently at some future time, please write to me, c/o Madame Wiola Paszkowska, 16 Grantley Terrace, London. (I no longer go to the Pavilion Hotel.) But I will not write to you again, ever again.*

*Coral Glynn*

Dolly was silent that night at dinner. Robin was aware that she often looked up from her plate and gazed at him across the table, but said nothing. "What's wrong?" he finally asked. "You seem preoccupied."

"Perhaps I am," said Dolly. "I was thinking about Coral. And how odd it is that she has never written to Clement."

"Odd?" asked Robin.

"Yes. Remember how she told us she would write to him, and send the letter here?"

"Of course," said Robin.

"And she has never written."

"No," said Robin. "Unless she sent the letter directly to Clement."

"But he told us, only last week, that he had heard nothing. And every time he sees me, he asks if a letter has arrived."

"Well, perhaps she sent him a letter breaking things off, and he is only keeping up the pretence."

"No," said Dolly. "Not Clement. He would tell us. Or you, certainly. It is odd."

"You can never know what is odd about other people," said Robin. "Things may appear odd, but that does not mean that they are. Usually there are very good reasons for things."

He paused, and as Dolly said nothing, he continued: "I imagine that once Coral arrived in London she decided she was well done with Clement. Their marriage made so little sense. You said so yourself."

"Yes," said Dolly. "It seemed odd to me. So much seems odd to me, even if what you say about odd things is true."

Robin said nothing.

"Odd and sad," said Dolly. "It is all very sad to me."

"I think it is best to forget about it. For Clement's sake."

"You are always thinking of Clement," said Dolly. "You are such a good friend to him. A dear friend."

Robin ducked his face and covered it with both hands.

Dolly sat quietly, observing him.

After a moment he lowered his hands and looked at her. His eyes shone and his cheeks were damp. "You found the letters," he said.

"Yes," said Dolly.

"Then why did you do that that? It isn't like you: it's cruel," Robin said. "Why did you play with me like that?"

"It is you that have been playing. I think it is all a game with you: your love for Clement, and for me. If you have any love. Is that how you see it? Feel it? Is it a game you are playing?"

"No," said Robin. "Of course not."

"I can imagine no other explanation," said Dolly.

"I am ashamed," said Robin.

"Yes," said Dolly, "at least there is that." She stood up and left the room, leaving Robin alone at the table. He sat there for a very long time, because there did not seem to be anything for him to do, or anywhere he could go.


When he finally did go upstairs to his bedroom, he saw that Dolly had left the letters on top of his dressing table. He realised that if he gave them to Clement now, it would be the end of their friendship. What a hard, unsatisfying word: "friendship." It was worth very little, friendship. It did not keep you warm at night. You could not even touch it. Friendship gave you a little bit of something you needed a lot of, slowly starving you, weakening you, breaking you down.

He took the letters into his bathroom and burnt them in the sink, where they left a charred mess of ashes, which he washed down the drain. And then he scrubbed the sink until there was no shadow left upon the porcelain, and washed his hands, and undressed, and put on his pyjamas, and got into bed, where he lay awake for a long time, not crying or feeling very much of anything—just a feeling of emptiness, a feeling of something—a light or a sound deep within him—going out, stopping, leaving him alone in the dark.

For a moment, when the front door of Hart House opened, Dolly did not recognise Mrs Prence. In the first place, she was dressed to go out, wearing a boldly, almost alarmingly green-and-gold-checked coat and a green felt hat with gold feathers in its brim. And she seemed quite alive, which was not a quality that Dolly had ever before associated with Mrs Prence, and so she was taken aback. Her gloved hand was pulled instinctively to her heart, and she gave a tiny gasp.

"Mrs Prence!" she exclaimed.

"Good afternoon, Mrs Lofting," Mrs Prence said, standing aside so that Dolly might enter the house.

"You are going out?" asked Dolly. It was a well-known fact that Mrs Prence shunned the world, and rarely emerged from the gloom within Hart House.

"I am going into town to have lunch with a friend," said Mrs Prence, as if it were something that happened every day. "You are here to see the Major, I assume?"

"I am," said Dolly. "Is he at home?"

"Of course," said Mrs Prence. "He goes nowhere. In the library all day, every day, staring at the four walls."

"Well, don't let me keep you," said Dolly. "I can find my own way."

"I'm in a hurry to catch the bus," said Mrs Prence, "as I don't want to be late for my appointment."

"Of course," said Dolly. "Enjoy your lunch. You are looking so well. For a moment I didn't recognise you."

"I don't think people change as much as all that," Mrs Prence enigmatically proclaimed, and hastened out the front door and down the steps.

Dolly removed her coat and gloves and scarf and laid them across a chair in the front hall. It was very quiet in the house, and the air smelt stale, as if it had all been breathed a few too many times. The door to the library was closed and she knocked upon it.

She heard Clement call, "Come in," and opened the door. He was sitting on a small sofa in a nook by the window. He wore a smoking jacket over an open-collared shirt, and she noticed there was ash down the front of it and some on the velvet seat of the sofa. He did not look up when she opened the door but continued staring out the window, which overlooked a few derelict outbuildings, and beyond them the water meadows. A marble ashtray on a little table in front of the sofa was full of cigarette butts, one of which, abandoned alit, continued to burn.

"Clement," she said, and then he did look over at her, and stood, and she said his name again, because he seemed unfocussed and in need of reminding who he was, and Dolly wondered what had happened, or was happening, at Hart House to cause its two inhabitants to become so unmoored from their heretofore resolute identities.

"Dolly!" he said, as if winning points for remembering her name.

She crossed the room and kissed him. His usual bracing antiseptic odour was replaced with a warm disagreeable funk, and she wondered when he had most recently bathed.

"Sit down, sit down," he said. "What a nice surprise. I was just

sitting here—" He looked around the room, obviously trying to find in its contents the suggestion of some recent activity, but, with the exception of the smoking cigarettes, there were no signs of life. "I was sitting here," he said, "waiting for you."

"I have just come for a little visit," said Dolly. "I was passing by and it occurred to me that I never see you alone, I must always share you with Robin, and I thought—I will drop in and have Clement all to myself for a moment or two."

Clement seemed not to know what to make of this confession, for he said, "Mrs Prence has just gone out. She is always going out these days. I think she is planning an escape."

"An escape? To where?"

"I don't know," said Clement. "She is very secretive. I think she has joined a band of witches. Or Gypsies. Or perhaps she will join the circus."

"What as?" asked Dolly.

"An orang-utan," said Clement. "Or perhaps a lion tamer. All she needs is a chair and a whip."

Dolly stubbed out the smoking cigarette. "You must put these out, Clement darling, or you'll burn down the house."

"That is precisely what I am trying to do," said Clement. "And now you've ruined it."

"Shall I go down and make us some tea?" said Dolly.

"I'd much rather a drink," said Clement.

"I think tea would be better. Sit down and don't do anything dangerous. I will be right back with a pot of tea."

When Dolly returned with the tea, Clement was once again seated upon the sofa, contemplating the scene outside the window. She moved the ashtray off of the little table, put the tray upon it, and poured. "Here," she said, holding one cup out for Clement, "give me that cigarette and drink this."

He handed her the cigarette, which she continued to smoke. He drank his tea thirstily and held out the cup for more. Dolly poured, and this time poured herself some as well.

"I look awful, don't I?" asked Clement.

"Yes," said Dolly. "As soon as I leave, you must go up and bathe and shave and brush your hair with tonic and splash eau de cologne all over yourself."

"I would have done so," said Clement, "had I known you were coming."

"It is awfully rude to just appear like this, I know," said Dolly, "but I did want to see you. There is something I want to tell you."

"Is there?" said Clement. "Have you heard from Coral?"

"No," said Dolly. "Or rather, yes."

"A letter? Did you bring it?"

"No," said Dolly.

"Why not?" said Clement. "You know I am mad to hear from her."

"Yes, I know," said Dolly. "I know that. And I thought that Robin did as well . . ."

"He did," said Clement. "Of course he did."

"Yes," said Dolly. "Of course he did. Which makes this all so much the stranger."

"What?"

"Apparently Coral wrote to you, as she said she would, as soon as was settled in London last spring. And then again, once or twice after that. I found the letters hidden in Robin's room. I was aghast, of course. I don't understand it. Or perhaps I do. Perhaps you do?"

"Robin?" said Clement.

"Yes," said Dolly. "Robin kept the letters from you. I found them quite by accident. I don't know what to say."

"But where are they?"

"The letters? They are gone. He burnt them."

"Did you read them?"

"Yes, I did. I could not help myself."

"Tell me! What did she write?"

"What she had promised to write: that she had arrived safely in London, and the address of the place she was staying. And then, in a second letter, a new address, of another place. And that she had got a job with the National Health—as a nurse, I suppose. And then in third and final letter she wrote that she was sorry for what she had done and understood why you did not want to see her again and that she would not write to you again. That is all I remember. I only read them once. And then Robin burnt them."

"Why? Why did you not save them for me?"

"I don't know," said Dolly. "I'm sorry. I left them for Robin, so that he could do right by you. I felt sure that he would. He had kept them from you, so it was for him to give them to you. But I misjudged him."

"Are you sure that he burnt them?"

"He told me that is what he did, and I believe him."

"But why? I don't understand. Why would he not give them to me? Why?"

"Oh, Clement," said Dolly. "You know. Of course you know."

Clement said nothing, so Dolly said it for him: "He loves you."

"But he shouldn't have done that," said Clement.

"Of course he shouldn't," said Dolly. "He knows it, too. He was ashamed and it was easier for him to complete his shame than to rectify it. He is weak. You know how weak he is, what a boy he is. And now he is despondent. He says he will emigrate."

"Emigrate? To where?"

"I don't know. Where does one emigrate these days? The Empire is dwindling as we speak. Canada or Australia, I suppose."

"Is he really leaving?"

"He says he is. And I think that, really, perhaps it is for the best."

"And you? Will you join him?"

"No," said Dolly. "I am not the emigrating type. I shall stay here. Or perhaps move to London. We shall separate."

"Oh, Dolly—"

"No. I think that is for the best as well."

"But you two always seemed to get along so well together."

"In a certain way, to a certain extent, we did. But that is not reason enough to stay together. Marriage is a tricky business."

"Yes," said Clement, "I know."

"Yours has certainly got off to a rocky start."

"But Coral wrote to me? You're sure?"

"Yes," said Dolly. "Of course I am sure."

"And when were the letters sent?"

"I told you: last spring. Soon after she left."

"And no more since then?"

"None that I saw. Or that Robin mentioned. I think he would have mentioned, if there were more."

"It is so long ago: last spring," said Clement.

"Hardly a year," said Dolly.

"She could have written to me here, and she has not," said Clement.

"You told her to send her letters to us."

"Yes, but if she had no response, she could have written to me directly. As a last resort."

"Perhaps she shall," said Dolly.

"Then I shall wait," said Clement.

"Wait?" said Dolly.

"What else can I do?"

"Surely something other than merely waiting."

"Do you think there is a chance Robin might not have burnt the letters?"

"I suppose there might, but I think he did. There is something so definite, so final, about his decision to emigrate. It suggests all bridges burnt. Or letters, in this case."

"Poor Robin," said Clement.

"No: poor Clement. Only you would feel sorry for Robin in these circumstances."

"But I do. I feel, somehow, that it is all partly my fault. Or perhaps entirely my fault. I should have let well enough alone. Now I have ruined Robin's life, and Coral's as well. And yours."

"I do not consider my life ruined, so you can remove my name from your list."

"But, Dolly . . . won't you miss him?"

"Of course I shall. But you see, as I have never completely had him, I have always missed him. Parts of him. Perhaps it is better to lose something entirely than to clutch at pieces of it."

"I suppose that is how Coral has come to think of me. Why she has let go."

"You do not know that she has."

"She knows where I am, and I do not know where she is. She could come to me or contact me at any time."

"Perhaps she is still afraid."

"Afraid? Of what?"

"Inspector Hoke. The girl in the woods."

"But all that is finished. They found the boy months ago. The case is closed."

"Yes, but does Coral know that? For all she knows, she may still be a suspect."

"I'm sure she knows. It was in all the newspapers, even the London ones."

Dolly stood up. "You surprise me, Clement. You are as weak as Robin. Such cowards, both of you."

"I don't know what you mean."

"Of course you don't. That is the saddest thing of all."

Dolly picked up the butt-heaped ashtray and stepped behind the sofa. She opened the window and emptied the ashtray onto the pachysandra in the garden below, and then, because the ashtray itself was still filthy, she chucked it out of the window. She stepped away and wiped her hands. "Leave the window open," she said. "The air in here is rather stale."

Clement stood, and appeared to be rather stunned by Dolly's visit, and by her recent words and actions. He said nothing.

"While I am here, telling you things, there is one more thing I think I should tell you."

"About Robin?"

"No. This is about Coral."

Clement said nothing. He shivered and put his hands in his jacket pockets. The air coming in the open window was very cold.

"Coral was pregnant when she left here. Did you know that?"

"No," said Clement. "She told you that?"

"Yes," said Dolly. "The morning of your wedding. She wanted to tell you, but I told her not to. I advised her to wait."

"Pregnant?" Clement said.

"Yes," said Dolly. "She was going to have a baby."

"Whose?" asked Clement.

"Apparently the man at her prior engagement had taken advantage of her. The pregnancy was a result of that misfortune."

"Ah, yes, she mentioned that—the unpleasantness."

"But not the result?"

"No," said Clement. "Why did you—do you—tell me now?"

"She is your wife," said Dolly. "And you seem reluctant to go to her. I thought that knowing this might rouse you to action."

"Did you? Really? It seems to me that it would have the opposite effect."

"What do you mean?"

"Informing me that my wife is pregnant with another man's child—hardly an incentive to go to her, is it? In fact, it is all too clear now why she was willing to marry me. I had thought—hoped—that it had something to do with love, but of course it had not, not at all. I was a fool."

"Oh, Clement," said Dolly. "You are really hopeless. You understand nothing." She leant forwards and brushed some of the ash from his gown. She kissed his cheek. She had done all that she could. "Good-bye," she said, and left him standing there, in the draft from the open window.

•

Clement had no idea if Robin would be at The Black Swan for their weekly meeting. If he knew that Dolly has informed me of his betrayal, he will not come, thought Clement. How could he? Had Dolly told him? She had left in such disgruntled haste, it was difficult to know what her feelings or intentions were.

Clement saw Robin enter the room and look across it towards the table in the inglenook that they always shared, and he knew immediately that Dolly had completed her mission, and that Robin knew that he knew. Robin looked like someone who had just been punched, and was waiting for further punishment.

He stood beside the table and Clement could not bring himself to look up at Robin's wounded face.

"Whiskey tonight, is it?" Robin asked. "Ready for another?"

"I suppose so," said Clement.

"I shall return," said Robin. He went up to the bar and returned with a whiskey and a pint of beer.

"No whiskey for you?" said Clement.

"No," said Robin. He sat down across from Clement. "I know you've had a visit from Dolly, and that she told you of my treacherous behaviour. I'm glad she did, in a way, because I couldn't tell you myself, and I've wanted to. But I was too weak to do that, too weak to do any but the wrong things."

"It isn't about weakness," said Clement.

"Oh, but it is. You don't know. I'm weak through and through, you see. The only brave thing I've ever done is coming to see you here tonight."

Clement said nothing.

Robin sipped his beer. After a moment he said, "It's funny, but I thought it was brave. I don't mean tonight; it isn't brave of me, I know. I mean what I did before—keeping the letters from you. I allowed myself to think it was brave to keep Coral's letters from you—even loyal, perhaps—because I thought I was protecting you from something. The cruel, cruel misunderstanding world and all that. But I didn't realise how I had it all wrong, how stupid I was. You don't love me, and you don't want my love. I'm sorry it's taken me so long to realise that; I know it's very stupid of me, because you've made it plain enough, time and again, and so of course in a way I had realised it, but I hadn't believed it. I couldn't believe it. It's hard not to believe in love. But I can now. It is all very clear to me now, and I'm sorry to have gone about something long after the fact of it—or maybe there was never even a fact of it; maybe it was always something I imagined. I don't know, I'll never know, but I'm sorry to have bothered you in all the ways I've bothered you. But it was only because—"

"Be quiet," said Clement. "Please stop."

"Yes: stop," said Robin. "That is what you have always wanted, haven't you, wanted me to stop. Well, I have. I am stopped now."

For a moment neither man spoke. Then Clement said, "Why do you make a melodrama of everything? There was no need for this."

"No need for what?"

"Any of this. This drama you have created."

"It's strange you use that word: 'need.' I wonder if you know anything about it. I don't think I have ever known you to need anything, or anyone. Have you?"

"Of course I have."

"What? Who?"

"I need the things that any man needs."

"Does that include love?" asked Robin. "Does it include sexual fulfilment?"

"I was thinking of more practical things. I have learned to do without a great deal."

"How?" asked Robin. "Will you teach me? Can you at least do that for me?"

"You have Dolly," said Clement.

"You know I don't have Dolly," said Robin, "not in the way we are speaking of. Not in the way of love, or sexual fulfilment."

"I wish you would stop saying these things."

"Why? Do they frighten you?"

"Of course they do not. It is simply neither the proper time or the place."

"And when and where would that be?" asked Robin.

"Is that why you destroyed my letters from Coral?"

"What do you mean?"

"Because you do not love Dolly, and are not fulfilled with her—is that why you did not want me to have Coral? Did you think that I might love her, and be fulfilled with her?"

"Oh, no. Quite on the contrary: because I know that you don't, and can't."

"And how do you know this?"

"Because you have just told me: you do not need, or want, these things yourself, so how could you ever give them to someone else?"

"Perhaps I could be taught. Perhaps I could learn. But now I shall not have the chance. You have seen to that."

"I don't think it's in your nature to love Coral," said Robin.

"You assume I am the same as you. At least in that respect."

"I know you are."

"And how can—do—you know this?"

"Because I love—loved—you. And because you loved me. Will you deny that?"

"No," said Clement. "I wish never to deny that. It was a part of my youth—the best part of my youth. But it is over. The man—the boy—you loved, and who loved you, no longer exists."

"You exist. I exist. Here we are together in The Black Swan, existing."

"But we are changed. I am changed."

"You are not changed. You only pretend to be changed. Because you are weak. You are the weak one, after all. Perhaps I have done wrong—I know that I have—but now I understand what I did was not done out of cowardice. Foolishness, yes, and selfishness, too, but the cowardice and cruelty is yours, it is all yours. And I would rather have done wrong out of love than done nothing from cowardice. How lonely and bitter and miserable you will be all your life, Clement, and do not think for a moment that Coral would have spared you any of that loneliness or bitterness or misery, because she would not have. She would have increased it a ten—a thousand—fold. That is a hell I have saved you from, and I am glad of that. It is my last and final way of loving you."

Robin stood up and walked out of the room, leaving Clement alone in the little nook by the hearth that they would never again share.

The reason that Dolly had found Major Hart in such an uncharacteristic state of *déshabillé* was a result of problems he had been having with his health. His skin had recently begun to crack and suppurate, causing him great pain and discomfort. Frequent bathing seemed to hasten his skin's disintegration, and the only clothes that felt comfortable were those of the loosest fit and softest material. Because he knew he was to blame for his worsening condition by refusing the skin grafts that had been suggested after the war, he put off seeing a doctor, and attempted to heal himself with assorted topical salves and unguents. And he tried to forget the stressful news that Dolly had brought him, but his efforts to forget only increased his strain, which in turn caused his condition to worsen, and become even more painful. When he could stand things no longer, he saw his doctor, who scoldingly reiterated his opinion that Clement should have had the skin grafts when they had been offered: he was not sure what treatment, if any, was now possible. The doctor sent him up to London to see an American doctor who specialised in burns. Dr Brown had invented a new instrument, the electrically powered dermatome, which harvested—for that was the term they used—skin for transplants.

But it was too late, Dr Brown told him: his dead skin would reject any transplant. It should have been done immediately, when the wounds were fresh. However, a colleague of his was experimenting with a pharmaceutically produced silk gauze that had proved successful in stabilizing critically burnt skin; apparently the gauze was so fine that it actually adhered to the dead skin and protected it from any further disintegration or infection. He was in Harley Street, and Dr Brown could arrange a consultation with him for the next day. If he wanted to go the National Health route, there was a dermatological clinic at St Mary's Hospital that might be able to offer some palliative help.

Clement left Dr Brown's office with an appointment to see Dr Tompkins the following afternoon, and walked out into the baked London streets. It was July, and very dry and hot: a fine dust hung in the sunlit air. Clement felt defeated; he had not expected to feel otherwise, although he had hoped, wildly, for a miracle. He always felt defeated by London: it was unknowable, and there was so much that could go, and be done, wrong. He decided he would stay at Durrants that night, because that was where his mother had always stayed when she went up to London, and see Dr Tompkins tomorrow—although, really, what was the use? Didn't one know when one had had enough?

Clement walked into Regent's Park, because although the lawns were mostly burnt, it did look slightly cooler and fresher in the park than on the busy street. He needed to sit in the shade for a while, just sit, and close his eyes, and separate himself from the world.

He saw Coral immediately upon entering the park, for she was sitting on a shaded bench beneath a towering catalpa tree just inside the entrance, wearing a nurse's costume. Whenever Clement saw a nurse, he thought of Coral, although he did not think of her as a nurse any longer—in an effort to dismiss her from his world, he had geographically and professionally exiled her, imagining that she must be a governess in France or a secretary in Philadelphia—and so to find her sitting there, in front of him, was shocking. It had not occurred to him that by coming to London he might encounter her, for he was not a man given to conjecture or speculation; for him life had happened and was only now being endured. He could not imagine the future as being anything except a continuation, or diminishment, of the present. He turned away and left the park.

When Coral returned to St Mary's Hospital that evening, the Sister told her that a man had come looking for her that afternoon. A gentleman, she said. He did not leave his name, and as the Sister who related the message was not the Sister who had spoke with him, he could not be described. But he had said that he would be at the hospital the following morning so he might see Coral before she began her rounds.

Of course it was Inspector Hoke; there was no one else it could be. More than a year had passed since Coral had left Harrington, and although she sometimes still dreamt of Hoke reappearing in her life, chasing after her through the rooms of a house or down the streets of some strange city, her conscious fear of him had abated, for she knew that if he had wanted to find her, he would have found her long ago. There must be new evidence, she thought, but what could it be?

The reappearance of Hoke aroused in her a fear that was irrational and wild, and caused her to forget that she had not been responsible for the death of the girl in the Sap Green Forest.

That night she did not sleep but sat in her room, feeling the world close down around her, the buildings of London collapsing like boxes, the trees in the squares retracting their branches and pulling themselves back into the earth, everything leaving, shutting down, abandoning her.

In the morning she bathed and dressed and left the house as if going to the hospital, but sat on a bench in the square, watching the door of 16 Grantley Terrace. She knew that when she did not appear at the hospital, Sister Castle would give Inspector Hoke her address, and so it would not be long before he arrived. Coral did not want to be arrested, or be questioned—or suffer any consequence of Hoke's reappearance—in Madame Paszkowska's house, for she had always been respected there, and treated well, and the thought of Miss Lingle abandoning Pansy and her chair so that she could step into the hallway and listen over the banister was too mortifying to contemplate.

She sat there all morning, watching, but no one approached number 16. About eleven o'clock she saw Madame Paszkowska close the windows in the drawing room and close the drapes, for it was getting very hot and the house stayed cooler when it was shut away from the heat of the day. A few moments later Madame Paszkowska reappeared in the bedroom windows on the second floor and repeated the ritual, and again on the third and fourth floors, until all the windows of the house were shut and shrouded, as if the house, like everything else, were leaving her, excluding her.

She fell asleep on the bench soon after that and awoke abruptly only moments later. A man was standing on the sidewalk outside of number 16. She looked at her watch, which was pinned upon her bodice and hung upside down, facing up, so that its time was private and revealed only to her. It was a thing she treasured, for it had been given to her by her parents when she had started nursing school. She was shocked to see that it was noon: she had slept for more than a few moments.

She stood and as if by instinct walked towards the iron fence that surrounded the square, stepping across the green forbidden lawn and pushing her way into the rhododendrons that grew inside the fence. Perhaps I am in a dream? she wondered. The heat beat down and everything shimmered, the bonnets of the cars parked along the street angrily throwing the sunlight back up into the sky, and through the crazed glare she watched the man climb the steps, grabbing hold of the rail and hoisting one leg up after the other, and it was by this strange gait that she realised it was Clement.

She wanted to call out, but something stopped her. Perhaps it was a feeling of disbelief, but it was incapacitating, as if the sense of folding up and shutting down she had experienced the night before

had finally progressed to her interior, and that she herself was being hollowed out, the bright noonday sun reaching in and scooping
her clean of everything. She could not move or speak, and in this
dreamlike trance she watched Clement ring the bell and straighten
and collect himself, fixing his cuffs and shrugging his linen jacket
close about his shoulders, and waiting, waiting, until Madame Paszkowska opened the door. Something prevented Coral from hearing
what they said to one another; it was not the distance, for she was
just on the other side of the road, and it was quiet on Grantley Terrace at midday. It was a great roaring that Coral heard, a sound that
started far away and grew louder and brighter as it approached, roaring at her from all directions, as strong and surrounding as the sun,
beating down upon her and yet, at the same time, lifting her up.


The ceiling in Madame Paszkowska's drawing room was high and
had, at one time, been elaborately plastered with dadoes, but much
of this decoration had plummeted during the Blitz. Coral stared up
at what was left, trying to make sense of it, but there were too many
gaps, too many missing pieces, and so it was impossible to imagine
the original design.

"Here," said Madame Paszkowska, leaning forwards with a
glass of water. "Drink this, my dear."

Coral continued to gaze at the ceiling, for she had the feeling
that she might, at any moment, see through it, if only she did not
look away—that it might open and reveal the sky, or another world.
But Madame Paszkowska was gathering her up and arranging her
so that she sat back upon the cushions of the sofa and the puzzling
ceiling disappeared.

"Drink this cool water," Madame Paszkowska said, and held
the glass up to Coral's lips. Coral drank a bit, and Madame Paszkowska lay a cool washcloth upon her brow.

And then, quite suddenly, it all returned to her, everything that had been disappearing, and she took the glass from Madame Paszkowska, and drank thirstily from it.

"She is better now, I think," said Madame Paszkowska, and Coral realised there was someone else in the room, and looked around to see Clement sitting in a chair in the shadows by the corner, looking as if he, too, had fainted. She knew the room was not very large, but nevertheless he appeared to be very far away, in another country, perhaps, a distant misty place.

"Clement," she said.

"Coral." He stood up. He was holding his hat in front of him with both of his hands, turning it around and around by its brim, as if he were trying to hypnotise her with it.

"Stop," she said.

He looked puzzled.

"Your hat," she said. "Stop spinning it."

"Oh," he said. He looked at his hat as if surprised to find it in his hands and then put it down upon the chair he had been sitting in. Then he showed Coral his empty hands, blank palms forward, to prove they were empty.

"I will go and make you some tea," said Madame Paszkowska. "This will be good for you both." She turned and left the room, pulling closed the doors behind her.

It was very quiet now, almost silent, just the ticking of the porcelain clock on the mantel atop which stood two silent Dresden shepherdesses.

After a moment Clement said, "Coral. It's a long time since I have seen you."

"Yes," she said. "A year—"

"Longer than that," he corrected. "It was April when you left."

"It was the beginning of the spring," Coral said. "I remember that."

"May I sit beside you?" he asked, after a moment.

Coral looked along the length of the sofa, which was strewn

with little silk pillows. Even in the dim submarine light the wooden floor glowed like the surface of a pond, so ferociously had its surface been waxed and buffed. The large gilt mirror on the mantel, inside of which the two shepherdesses faced away into another reality, as if turning their backs on this world, reflected a single shard of light that fell through a chink in the drapes back into the room. Coral moved two of the pillows nearer to her, opening a space on the sofa apparently intended for Clement. This was as close as she could come to inviting him to sit beside her.

He sat, and they both faced forwards, staring across the room at the drapes that hung in shadowed folds against the large front windows, and then Clement stood up and walked over and adjusted the drapes so that the wand of light that had entered the room was exiled. Then he sat back down, this time turning a bit towards Coral, and crossed his legs. Finally, he turned a bit more and looked at her. "So, you are still a nurse?" he asked.

As she was dressed in her nurse's uniform, there could be little doubt as to her occupation, unless she had become theatrically inclined, but she let this idiocy of his pass and said, "Yes, I am."

"Of course you are," he said. "You must forgive me, I'm feeling a bit addled. Are you all right? You fainted dead away—"

"I am feeling fine now," said Coral. "It was only the heat."

"Would you like me to go away?"

"No," said Coral. "Madame Paszkowska is bringing tea," she added, as if this were the reason why he should stay.

"She is very kind," said Clement.

"Yes," said Coral. "I am very lucky here. Very lucky indeed."

"How are you Coral? How is your life?"

"Oh," said Coral. "I am very well. Everything is fine."

"Do you still work as a private nurse?"

"No," she said. "I'm a visiting nurse, with the NHS."

"So you still visit people in their homes?"

"Yes," she said. "Mostly diabetics, but only briefly." She paused for a moment and then said, "I prefer it that way."

"I am sorry if I shocked you, coming here like this. I should have written to you here first, but I only learned your address this morning."

"Oh, no . . ." said Coral. "It wasn't you who shocked me. I thought you were Hoke."

"Hoke?"

"Inspector Hoke. I thought he had come to arrest me, or to ask me questions."

"Arrest you for what?"

"The girl that was hanged in the woods," said Coral.

"Don't tell me you have worried about that," said Clement. "That was solved ages ago, soon after you left. They found that it was a little boy, just as you said. It was an accident—they were playing some game in the woods. I hoped you might have read about it in the newspapers."

Coral said nothing.

"Did you?" he asked.

"No," she said. "I did not."

"I'm so sorry," he said. "I suppose I did the wrong thing, suggesting you go away . . ."

"No," she said.

"I was frightened for you," he said.

"Yes," she said. "I was frightened, too. It was right for me to leave there. And right for you to not answer my letters. It all happened, I think, as it ought."

"No," said Clement. "No! It has all gone wrong. Oh, Coral! Robin kept your letters from me. I only found out about them recently. Dolly found them. I thought that you had not written to me."

"Well, whatever happened, I think we both saw right to give it up. How it happened does not really matter. Besides, it is all in the past. Everything has happened as it ought."

"How fatalistic you are, Coral. I wish that I could feel the same."

"You don't?"

"No," said Clement. "I don't. I don't know what I feel, really, but I know that I don't feel that everything has happened in the proper way. In fact, I feel that very little has happened as it ought, at least in my life. I do not blame the gods, however. The fault is all mine."

"It is no one's fault. Robin's, perhaps, but we cannot blame him."

"I can blame him. And I do."

"How is Robin? How is Dolly?"

"They are separating—divorcing, perhaps; I'm not sure. Robin is going to Australia."

"Australia?"

"Yes," said Clement. "He wants to start a new life there, and Dolly, I think, will move here to London. I suppose she will start a new life, too."

"So many new lives," said Coral.

"It is absurd," said Clement. "They are both absurd."

"Oh, no," said Coral. "On the contrary. I think they are both very brave. And Mrs Prence? How is she?"

"Ah," said Clement. "A miracle has occurred in that quarter. You will not believe it."

"What?"

"Mrs Prence has begun a new life, too. She has married. Or remarried, I suppose."

"To whom?"

"To your old friend, Inspector Hoke. He came to the house several times after you left, while the enquiry was on-going. And somehow a romance—or friendship—was born. I know it sounds preposterous, but it is true."

"I don't think it's preposterous at all," said Coral. "It makes very good sense to me."

"Does it? I found it all quite mystifying."

"Yes, but love is mystifying," said Coral. "That is why it makes perfect sense."

Clement said nothing.

"Poor Clement! Who looks after you now? Is there a new Mrs Prence?"

"No," said Clement. "There is, thank God, only one Mrs Prence. I am alone at Hart House now. A girl comes daily and cleans a bit and cooks something inedible for me. She is paid twice as much as Mrs Prence and does half the work, if that."

"Well, I am glad to know that Mrs Prence is happy. At least someone is."

Clement turned to her. "Are you?" he asked.

"Happy? Yes, I am, sometimes. Mostly, I suppose. There is no reason for me not to be happy."

Clement did not reply for a moment but then said, "Dolly told me something else as well."

"What was that?" asked Coral.

"She told me—she said that you had told her—that you were going to have a child."

"Yes," said Coral. "I did tell her that."

"And was it true?"

"Yes," said Coral. "It was true. I was going to tell you that night—the night we were married—but other things happened. And I knew that it was too late to tell you, in any case. I'm sorry that I deceived you."

"Oh, no," he said. "No. I understand. How difficult things were for you then."

Coral said nothing. She looked down at her hands. She was still wearing her white gloves, but they were both grimed—from when she had fainted in the square, no doubt. She took them off and tossed them onto the little table that stood before the sofa. They rested upon one another, two little twisted hands trying to clutch.

"And did you— How is the child?" Clement asked.

"The child?"

"Yes," he said. "Your child."

"Oh," she said. "Oh—no. The child is gone."

He was not sure what she meant by this. "I'm so sorry," he said.

Coral said nothing for a moment, and then reached out for her gloves, shook the frozen gesture out of them, and rolled one tightly inside the other, then put the little ball of them on the floor, as if there were something shamefully intimate and untoward in their public display.

"How did you find me?" she asked. "How did know to come here?"

"I came up to London yesterday to consult a doctor about my—my skin. I've been having some troubles. And he mentioned the National Health, and I remembered Dolly had said that you were working for them; it was one of the few things she remembered from your letters. You see, she read them before Robin destroyed them. Fortunately. Or perhaps not. In any case, I thought I would go the hospital and try to find out about you, see if I could find you. And it was quite easy, as the Sister told me you worked out of St James, and would be there in the morning.

"So I returned to the hospital this morning, and when you did not appear, the Sister was worried. She said it was unlike you to miss work. She telephoned here, and your landlady told her that you had left this morning as usual, which caused the Sister to be even more concerned. I asked her for your address, so that I might come and try to find you. At first she would not tell me, for she said it was against regulations, but then I remembered something that changed everything. Do you know what I remembered?"

"No," said Coral.

Clement waited a moment, but when Coral said no more, he continued. "I remembered that we were married. That you were my wife. And that therefore I was entitled to be told where you lived. Fortunately, I had our writ of marriage with me, and I showed that to the Sister." He reached into his jacket pocket and withdrew the folded certificate, which he carefully unfolded. He lay it upon the table recently occupied by Coral's gloves. Because of the way it had been folded, and perhaps pressed against his warm breast, the corners of the paper lifted away from the table, and like a paper bowl it rested daintily upon the point where the four creases met. Clement reached out his large hand and smoothed the paper against the table's marble surface, but as soon as he raised his hand, the paper lifted its edges away from the table once again, yet less wilfully.

"She could see then, the Sister, that there was no regulation keeping her from telling me where you lived, and she did so: sixteen Grantley Terrace, she said, and very kindly said she thought it was near the Gloucester Road."

Coral said nothing; she seemed somewhat stunned by Clement's speech, or perhaps it was the lingering effects of her recent collapse. She stared blankly at the paper on the table before them for a moment, and then said, "But why—why did you want to see me?"

"I don't know," said Clement. "It's all very confusing, of course, everything that's happened, and I didn't know what to think."

"You thought I hadn't written to you?" asked Coral.

"Yes. Well, of course I did. What else could I think? I asked Dolly and Robin every time I saw them if a letter from you had come, and they always said no. Of course I believed them. Robin, especially. He was my friend."

"They didn't like me," said Coral. "I thought you knew that."

"Of course they liked you. They both told me so in no uncertain terms."

"Yes, but don't you see now that they lied to you? As they did about the letters?"

"Only Robin lied. Dolly did not know about the letters. As soon as she found them, she told me."

"How do you know?"

"How do I know what?"

"How do you know that she told you as soon as she knew about them? I'm sure she knew about them all along. They were sent to her house, after all."

"Why did you not write to me directly when you had no response?"

"Because you told me to write to Dolly and Robin. I was doing what you wanted, what you told me to do. And then when you didn't answer, I assumed you had never intended to. And I saw then that our marriage was a mistake, done in some sort of desperation on both our parts, I think, and was best forgotten."

"Oh, Coral," said Clement. "Do you still feel that way?"

"Of course I do," said Coral. "As time passes, it only becomes clearer." She reached out and touched the paper on the table before them. "I suppose we should do something about this," she said.

"What?" asked Clement.

"We should divorce," said Coral. "There is no reason for us to stay married now."

"Oh," said Clement. "Yes. I suppose. Have you—is there someone else you would like to marry?"

"Oh, no," said Coral. "I did not mean that. No. I want never to marry again. I was thinking of you."

"Well, I shall never marry again. Marrying once was apparently more than I could manage."

"You just married the wrong person," said Coral. "Think of Mrs Prence. You have only to meet your Inspector Hoke." She laughed.

"I'm sorry, but I do not find that funny, Coral, not funny at all. I did not marry the wrong person. Did you?"

"Oh, Clement—I'm sorry. I didn't mean to make a joke of anything. Really, I didn't. I just don't know what to think—how can I? You cannot appear like this, and tell me these things, and expect me to know what to think or say. It's all such a muddle."

"Yes," he said. "Of course, you're right." He took the certificate off of the table, carefully folded it along its creases, and returned it to the pocket inside his jacket. "And I am sure you are right about ending our marriage as well. Forgive me for not having better sense about that. You know how stupid I am about these things."

He stood up.

"Clement," said Coral. "Don't go. Please sit down again."

"No," said Clement. "You should lie down. I have upset you

enough already. And besides, I have an appointment in Harley Street. The doctor I saw yesterday suggested I consult a colleague, who will no doubt pass me along to yet someone else. That seems to me all doctors are good at. I would do much better, I think, to simply take the train home."

Clement stood there for a moment, considering.

"Of course you should go and see the doctor," said Coral.

"I don't suppose . . ." said Clement, but halted.

"You don't suppose what?" asked Coral.

"Oh, nothing," he said. "No." But then he turned to her. "I was only wondering if, perhaps, this evening—"

He halted again, and this time Coral did not prompt him. "It was only that I wondered if you might dine with me this evening. If I go to see this other doctor now, as you suggest, instead of going home, I will be alone in the city tonight, which is something I don't enjoy. It would mean so much to me if you would join me. Unless, of course, you have other plans, which I suppose you must."

"No," said Coral. "I have no plans."

"I'm staying at Durrants. I believe the food they serve is acceptable, but I would happily take you anywhere. I'm afraid I don't know anything about restaurants in London. But I should so like to hear about your life here."

Coral said nothing.

"Do you know Durrants?" Clement asked.

"No," said Coral.

"It is in Manchester Square," said Clement.

Coral turned to him and said, "I only said that I had no plans this evening. I said nothing about anything else."

He looked puzzled for a moment, as if she were speaking in some language he was a student of, and comprehended only with delaying effort. Then her meaning seemed to pierce him. He winced and said, "Of course. I'm sorry. I misunderstood you."

Suddenly a loud roar came from the street, and they both

heard the windows battered. Clement walked across the room and drew back one of the drapes. The world had gone terribly dark, and it was pouring with rain outside, too much rain all at once, as unconvincing as in a film.

Coral rose from the couch and came and stood beside Clement. There was something wonderful about the rain, the force of it, and the amazing quickness with which the day went from light to dark. They stood there, side by side, watching the rain pelt the pavement of Grantley Terrace, watching the drops smack the street and splash upwards, the mesmerizing confusion of it, the movement down followed so quickly, so impossibly quickly, by the movement up.

Coral sat at her open window looking down into the garden, waiting for it to be time to walk across the park and have dinner with Clement at Durrants.

She had bathed and was wearing her best dress, which was still the navy blue with white polka dots she had worn to visit Walter DeVries. The only difference was she had a navy blue bag now, which was much better with the dress than the black.

A woman entered the next-door garden and emptied rubbish into a bin, then lit a cigarette. She stood there smoking, basking in the early evening light. The rain had stopped, leaving an almost cool freshness behind. Coral watched the smoke from the woman's cigarette drift up into the lighted air.

Someone knocked on the door and Coral called out, "Come in."

Madame Paszkowska opened the door. Coral stood.

"Coral," Madame Paszkowska said, "how pretty you look. What a pretty dress."

"Thank you," said Coral.

Madame Paszkowska stood in the doorway, as if uncertain why she was there. "Are you feeling better?" she finally asked.

"Yes," said Coral. "I am feeling fine now. It is a lovely evening."

They both looked at the open window. "Yes," said Madame Paszkowska, "how I love these summer evenings." She said nothing more, but continued to gaze out of the window at the pale blue sky.

After a moment Coral said, "What is it? Is something wrong?"

"Oh," said Madame Paszkowska. "I am afraid—I think I did do something wrong this afternoon."

Coral waited for her to continue, and when she did not, Coral said, "What did you do?"

"This afternoon, when you were in the drawing room with your friend, do you remember I said I would bring you tea?"

"Yes," said Coral. "I remember."

"Well, I did, but instead of bringing it into the room, as I should have done, I am afraid I stood outside the door and listened to your conversation."

"Oh," said Coral.

"I am very sorry," said Madame Paszkowska. "I know it was a wrong thing to do. And I am not in the habit of, how do you say—eardropping?"

"Eavesdropping," said Coral.

"Oh." Madame Paszkowska seemed doubtful, but continued. "And so I learned that your friend—that man—he is your husband. That you are married, no?"

"Yes," said Coral.

"Of course I am surprised. You have never mentioned to me that you are married."

"No," said Coral. "I have not."

"It is all very confusing, I know. All of our lives. But I learn this about you today, and now I do not know what to do . . ."

"About what?" asked Coral.

"I know—I cannot help but know—that you and Lazlo have been . . . *intime.* And I think that perhaps, I could be wrong, but yet I think that you may have some love for Lazlo."

Madame Paszkowska paused, but Coral did not respond. It was almost as if she had not been listening to what Madame Paszkowska said.

"Oh, Coral!" exclaimed Madame Paszkowska. "I do not know what is right or wrong. I only want to help you, because I have such warm feeling for you, and you seem to be so alone. Is this man today your husband?"

"Yes," said Coral. "But not really."

"I do not understand."

"Neither do I," said Coral. "Not really. We were married to each other before I came to London. But it was an odd marriage."

"Many marriages are odd," said Madame Paszkowska. "I myself have had two."

"Mine was very odd," said Coral. "It lasted a day. Less than a day."

"But you will be together again, now that he has found you?"

"I don't know," said Coral.

"Is it because of Lazlo that you do not go back to him?"

"No," said Coral. "It has nothing to do with Lazlo."

"That is what I worry," said Madame Paszkowska. "I worry that perhaps you think Lazlo— I do not know what Lazlo has told you, if you know that he is engaged to be married."

"No," said Coral. "I did not know."

"A girl he has met on holiday in Lowestoft. She is a nice girl, from a good French family, he says. Her name is Yvonne Marchand. They will marry in September."

Coral closed her eyes. She cannot be from a very a very good family if she spends her holiday in Lowestoft, she thought. She opened her eyes and reached out and straightened the painting that hung on the wall, the painting of the two red-breasted robins perched upon the rim of their nest. Then she sat upon her bed. "Why do you tell me this?" she asked Madame Paszkowska. "I don't think it concerns me."

"If I am unwelcome, please forgive me," said Madame Paszkowska. "It was wrong, perhaps, to speak to you of this. But I was not sure, all afternoon, I wonder what I should do, what I should say, or if I should do, say, nothing, and I think it is best to say these things because they may mean something to you, but you must forgive me if I have done the wrong thing."

"No," said Coral. "You have been very kind. And I am very happy for Lazlo and Yvonne. And how happy you must be!"

"Lazlo is bad sometimes, but I love him."

"He was not bad to me," said Coral. "You must not think that. He was good to me."

"Oh, Coral . . . What will you do? He seems such a nice man, your husband. Surely you will go and be with him now. This is no life for you."

"What do you mean?" asked Coral.

"I mean here, in this room, in this house. Going out every day as you do, taking care of strangers. I do not think that is a good life for you. Do you not want a home, and children?"

"I don't know," said Coral. "I don't know what I want. But I like my life. Here, in this room, in this house. Taking care of strangers."

"I do not think it is a life for a woman like you. You will finally be like Miss Lingle, with her rabbit."

"Miss Lingle seems very happy to me," said Coral. "I could do much worse."

"Yes, of course, but you could also do much better. Now is your chance for a proper life."

"A proper life? What is a proper life?"

Madame Paszkowska crossed the room and sat beside Coral on the bed. She reached out and patted Coral's hair, smoothed it, and held her hand gently against Coral's head.

"You seem so lost, so unhappy," said Madame Paszkowska. "What is the problem with this man? He seems to love you, I think. Do you love him?"

Coral said nothing. She did not realise she was crying until Madame Paszkowska wiped the tears from her cheek.

"What did he do, that you run from him? Did he beat you?"

"Oh, no," said Coral. "No. He was good to me. I always felt safe with him."

"Then why? Why do you leave him, and come here to London, and be alone?"

"I told you," said Coral. "It was all a mistake. A muddle. We were both scared, frightened—"

"Frightened? Of what?"

"I can't explain it all," said Coral. "It was like a dream, a bad dream, and now it is over. Or I thought it was, until he appeared today." She stood up and looked out the window.

"It is not over," said Madame Paszkowska. "It has hardly begun."

"No," said Coral. "It is over. Or perhaps it never was."

"Did you not ever love him?"

"I don't know," said Coral.

"I think you did. You must have. Otherwise, why would you wear that dress? Why would you look so beautiful?"

"I don't," said Coral. "And this is my only dress."

"It is not. You have several dresses. I have seen them. None is like this. You always look very pretty, yes, but not like this. So you must feel something if you wear this dress."

Coral said nothing.

"You said he was good to you. And that you felt safe with him. No?"

"Yes," said Coral. "But that is not love."

"Is it not? How do you know? Do you know what love is?"

"No," said Coral.

"I think you do," said Madame Paszkowska. She got up and stood in the doorway. She turned and smiled at Coral. "Of course you do," she said. She left the door open behind her.

Coral looked out the window. The woman had left the garden next door, and the sun had fallen behind some distant buildings.

•

Clement sat in the lobby of Durrants. The grating noise of mirth flowed out of the dining room. It was far past the expected hour, and there was obviously no point in him sitting there any longer, abandoned, on display, but he could not bear the thought of returning to his room, or the prospect of dining alone. He had engaged a table for two and asked for a chilled bottle of Sancerre to be waiting.

A maid came through the lobby and turned on the lamps: it was getting dark. The porter asked him, for the second time, if he was waiting for a taxi. He shook his head and then got his key and went up to his room. He left the lights turned off and crossed the room to the window, where an artificial brightness from the world outside dully shone.

He sat on the bed. He wanted to get out of the hotel but he had no idea where he could go. He supposed he could try to get a train home—it was still relatively early—but he realised the idea of arriving at Hart House in the small dark hours of the morning was as unbearable as staying where he was.

In fact, he suddenly realised, there was nowhere he could bear to be.

He got up and opened the closet. The rod was too low, and his weight would break it in any case. He wished he had brought his gun with him, but of course he had not. That left his razor.

He turned then and looked at the window, at the night light falling through the net curtain, and listened for a moment to the sounds that rose up from the street. A woman's laughter—laughter!—and automobiles passing in front of the hotel. He crossed the room and shut the windows and pulled the drapes closed and then it was dark in the bedroom, and almost silent. He removed his jacket and his shoes and socks. He undid his tie and then undressed completely. He turned on the light in the bathroom only long enough to find his razor and balance it on the rim the tub, and then he went back and turned the light off. It was completely dark then and he felt his way across the room to the tub. It was old, deep and long, and he stepped up into it and then lay down along the porcelain, and felt the coolness of it against his naked flesh. It was the right time and the right place. He felt certain about it, and for a moment there was something positive about this surety that confused him, that made him think perhaps he was wrong. But no—that was a trick. He was sure. He lay very still in the dark, letting the feeling of surety well up inside him.

After a moment he heard someone walking along the corridor, towards his door, and he thought: Coral has come; she has changed her mind. He sat up and listened to the steps come closer and then stop outside his door.

While hoisting himself out of he tub, he knocked his razor to the floor. He heard it skitter across the ceramic tiles and stepped upon it while searching for the light. It seemed blindingly bright in the bathroom when he had turned it on, and the knocking on the door sounded extremely loud, as if his nakedness exposed him too vulnerably to the assaulting world.

He stood there for a moment, confused, dazed by the light and the sound and the sharp pain he suddenly felt on the sole of his foot where the razor had cut him, and then he heard the knock again and realised it was not Coral at the door, not Coral at all: the knock was far too brisk and bold to have come from her.

"Who is it?" he called.

"Major Hart?" A young man's voice: the porter. "I have message for you. A note."

"I'm in the bath. Slip it beneath the door."

"Yes, sir," the porter said, and Clement heard the sound of paper being pushed beneath the door, but the carpet inside the room prevented it from entering.

"It won't go," said porter. "The carpet or something is stopping it. Can you open the door, sir?"

Clement realised he did not want the message in the room. "No," he said. "Read it to me."

"Sir?"

"The message. Please read it to me."

"I believe it's a private message, sir."

"Of course it is. Just read it."

He waited but heard nothing. "I can't hear you," he said.

"I'm opening the envelope, sir. It says, 'I am terribly sorry, but I think we both know it is not meant to be. Better to stop now. Coral.'"

After a moment the porter said, "Did you hear, sir? Would you like me to read it again?"

"No," said Major Hart. "I heard. Thank you." He felt his foot slip against the floor and looked down to see the blood.

"Will you still be wanting your table, sir?"

"What?"

"The table you reserved in the dining room. Mr. Simpson, the maître d', wonders will you still be wanting it, sir?"

"No," said Clement.

"Very good, sir. Is there anything else?"

"Could you bring me a bandage or something? I've cut my foot."

"A bandage, sir? Are you bleeding?"

"Yes," said Clement. "I am."


The following morning, before she left the house, Coral found Madame Paszkowska reading the morning paper in her private sitting room.

"Good morning," she said.

"Coral!" cried Madame Paszkowska. "Come in. Sit down."

"No," said Coral. "I'm late for work. I've only come to tell you that I will be leaving Grantley Terrace at the end of the month. I want to give you proper notice."

Madame Paszkowska smiled at her. "So, you will be joining your husband after all?"

"No," said Coral.

"No? But why? I thought—"

"I will be staying here in London," said Coral, "but I must leave Grantley Terrace."

"Buy why, Coral, why? What has come over you? What has happened?"

"Nothing has happened. Nothing at all. I just don't feel it is right for me to live here any longer, under the circumstances."

"There are no circumstances. Do you mean Lazlo? He will not be here again until Christmastime."

"I will not want to be here then, so it is best for me to leave now. I have thought it all over, and I am sure I am doing the best thing."

"But you must not leave, Coral, you cannot! Oh, what have I done? I see now I was wrong to speak to you yesterday, it is always wrong to interfere, I should have kept my tongue still in my head. Oh, please, Coral, forget everything I told you. I wanted to help you, but I see now I was wrong."

"Oh, no," said Coral. "No. You did help me. You did. If it weren't for you, I might have . . ."

"What? What might you have done?"

"I might have behaved foolishly," said Coral. "For a second time."

Madame Paszkowska got up from her sofa and came to Coral, and held her in her arms. Then she stood back and touched Coral's cheek. "I do not accept this. You must think. Don't worry about proper notice or anything like that. We decide nothing now. You stay here as long as you want. It is your home. Promise me you will think."

"I have thought," said Coral. "I am sure. I will leave at month's end."

Clement and Coral's marriage was legally and amicably terminated in 1954, on the basis of three years' desertion.

# PART FIVE

They had left London early and had driven all morning, travelling north along the smooth new motorway. Lazlo had bought special gloves, which revealed a square of bare flesh on the back of each of his hands, and special shoes, whose supple leather soles were stippled with bumps, for their trip, as if they were going on a safari or some special expedition, not simply driving to Yorkshire. But his vanity was good-natured and enjoyable. It was one of the many things Coral loved about him.

He was also a very good driver, and Coral liked that as well. Lazlo drove fast, deftly weaving in and out of the traffic, passing almost every car they encountered, as if they alone had a future.

Coral did not think about stopping in Harrington—indeed, she did not know they would be passing by Harrington—until she saw sign proclaiming its distance from them.

"Harrington," she said.

Neither of them had spoken in over an hour. He took one of his hands off the steering wheel, reached over, and grasped her hand.

"What silly gloves," she said.

"I like them," he said. "What did you say?"

"Harrington," she repeated. She touched the skin in the window of his glove.

"What is Harrington?"

"We just passed a sign. It is a town, ahead of us. Twenty miles. I lived there once."

"In your nursing days?"

"Yes," said Coral. "In my nursing days."

"Who was your patient?"

"An old lady, dying of cancer."

"Sounds very cheery," said Lazlo.

Coral turned and looked out the window. "It was nearly fifteen years ago," she said. "Imagine that. The spring of 1950. A very wet spring."

"All springs are wet," said Lazlo.

"That spring was especially wet."

"Does it have a decent restaurant? It is about time we stopped for lunch."

"It's were I met Clement," said Coral.

"My God!" said Lazlo. "No wonder you remember it. The famous Clement. My predecessor."

"No," said Coral. "He wasn't that."

"Then what was he?"

"I don't know," said Coral. "I don't think I shall ever know what he was. You are the one with a proper predecessor. Or rather, I am: Yvonne."

"Less said, best forgotten," said Lazlo, which is what he always said when Yvonne was mentioned. "Shall we stop? Perhaps we shall find your Clement. I should very much like to see him."

"There is a place for lunch," said Coral. "At least, there was."

"Then of course there still is," said Lazlo. "These provincial towns never change."


They drove along the High Street. The flower shop was still there, but Dalrymple's Better Dresses had become a greengrocer's. The Black Swan remained The Black Swan, and very little about it seemed to have changed, including the menu. It being summer, melon was in season.

"A dismal lunch," Lazlo announced as their table was cleared. "We shall do much better at Hatton Hall."

"That remains to be seen," said Coral.

"Really, Coral, how can you doubt it? Ye of little faith."

"It's not your abilities I doubt," said Coral. "I know you can do better than this, but the place isn't ours yet."

"Formalities," said Lazlo. "Simply a matter of formalities. I know it shall be."

"Formalities and money," said Coral. She stood. "I'm returning to the ladies'."

"I'll meet you outside, then. I want to look around for your corporal."

"He was a major," said Coral.

"An old duffer with a gamey leg, at any rate," said Lazlo. "He should be easy enough to spot."

Coral leant down and kissed him. "Don't make fun," she said.

Lazlo watched her walk across the dining room and disappear into the lounge. He paid the bill and then went through the lounge and out into the little garden that stood between the Swan and the street. It was overcrowded with hollyhocks and lilies and all the other tiresome flowers expected in an English garden. If it were his, he would tear them all out and do something very modern and elegant: a lawn and miniature privet with a white gravel border. Perhaps some topiary. He lit a cigarette and strolled up the walkway and stood in the sun on the sidewalk along the High Street.

A large woman in a flowered dress whose pattern echoed the garden he had just passed through stood behind a little table in front of the tobacconist's next door. "Come here and buy a flower," she called to him, holding out a tin filled with different-coloured tissue-paper poppies. "It's for a very good cause."

Lazlo ambled over to her. "Good afternoon," he said.

"Good afternoon," the woman said. "Will you buy a flower? Or several? A half crown each. They make very nice boutonnieres, and I can't help noticing that you are without one."

"What's it for?"

"Spastic children. St Hilda's Hospital. We're building a new ward."

"What colour?" asked Lazlo.

"Red, I think." She picked a red posy from the can and held it against Lazlo's lapel. "Or pink, perhaps. I don't know." She repeated the procedure with a pink flower. "What do you think?"

"The pink, I'd say."

"Yes," the woman said. "The red is too bold. The pink suits you perfectly." She tucked the flower into his buttonhole. "There," she said. "And one for the lady as well?"

Lazlo turned to find that Coral was standing beside him. "Do you like my flower?" he asked. "It's for a children's hospital."

"Very pretty," said Coral. "I'll have the red one, please."

"Lovely," said the woman. She handed Coral the red flower.

"Dolly?" Coral asked. "It is you! I thought it was."

"Coral!" said Dolly. "My stars! Can you imagine—Coral!"

"I take it you two know one another," said Lazlo.

"Yes," laughed Coral. "This is Dolly Lofting. And, Dolly, this is my husband, Lazlo Paszkowski."

"How do you do," said Dolly.

"Very pleased to meet you," said Lazlo.

"Dolly and her husband were close friends of Clement's," said Coral.

"We stood with you at your wedding," said Dolly. "Do you remember?"

"Of course I do," said Coral. "How is Robin?"

"I don't really know, to tell you the truth. Our marriage ended. He has moved away from here."

"That's right—to Australia, wasn't it?"

"Oh, no," said Dolly. "That was just one of his fancies. He got only as far as Brighton. He runs an antique store there called The Gilded Age, with a gentleman friend. The contents of Eustacia Villa comprise the lion's share of their inventory."

Coral turned to Lazlo. "Dolly and Robin had the most wonderful house, full of beautiful things."

"Most of it was junk, I'm afraid," said Dolly, "but I suppose most so-called antiques are. And of course you never know what's what in Brighton."

"But don't you miss all your lovely things?" asked Coral.

"Not at all," said Dolly. "I have never been sentimental about objects. It seems such a waste of feeling to me."

"But you had such unusual furniture," said Coral. "I remember your house so well. It must seem quite empty without it."

"Oh, Coral," said Dolly. "Didn't you know? I was sure you did."

"Know what?"

"How funny, how odd, life is: I live at Hart House now. I'm married to Clement. I imagined you knew, but of course how could you, as we've lost touch."

"Dolly—are you really? Married to Clement?"

"It's been several years—since '56. It just suddenly made sense you know, in the most wonderful way possible. We have been very happy together."

"I'm so happy for you, Dolly—and for Clement as well," said Coral.

"I feel somehow we are all related," said Lazlo. "How jolly it is."

"You are too charming," said Dolly, adjusting his pink boutonniere. "But what on earth are you doing here, in Harrington? Are you here to see Clement? Is something wrong?"

"Oh, no," said Coral. "Not at all. We are just motoring north from London and thought we would stop here for luncheon. I didn't realise the motorway passed so near to Harrington."

"That blasted motorway!" said Dolly. "It will change everything, they say. They're about to drain the water meadows and build modern villas. Who shall live in them, no one knows. Can you imagine— Hart House surrounded by semidetached villas? They wanted to buy our land, too, but of course Clement wouldn't allow it. We've put in a new kitchen—it's no longer in the basement—and also refitted the lavs. So we're no longer in the Dark Ages, although there's still lots to do. Nothing had been done in that house forever, as you know." Dolly turned to Lazlo. "A mausoleum," she said, "an absolute mausoleum. But you must come and see it. You must. And Clement, too, of course."

"Oh, no," said Coral. "We haven't time, I'm afraid. We need to be in Yorkshire this evening. We're hoping to a buy a property there, a country house. For a hotel. Lazlo manages hotels."

"I adore hotels," said Dolly. "I would live in one if I could. I shall come and stay immediately you're open. But, Coral darling, you simply can't just pop off after appearing like this! I forbid it. You must come and have tea with us. And stay the night if you can. Surely you can arrive in Yorkshire in the morning! Nothing will happen to your country house overnight."

"It's very kind of you," said Coral, "but we must be there this evening."

"Well, what about on your way home? Surely you could stop with us then?"

"Perhaps," said Coral. "We'll see."

"Well, I hope you shall. Oh, Coral, I'm overcome, really I am, to see you. I must embrace you, I must."

Dolly leant forwards and pulled Coral into her embrace, and when she released her, Coral saw that there were tears in Dolly's eyes. "I've always been so fond of you, really I have, you were such a dear, darling thing. You seemed so lost and afraid, and I wanted to help you, really I did."

"And you did," said Coral. "You were very kind to me, Dolly. And I am so happy to know that you and Clement are married. Very happy indeed."

"Are you?" asked Dolly. "I do adore him, you know. But I would never want you to think—"

Coral reached out and touched Dolly's arm. "I'm very happy

for you both," she said. "And now, really, we must be getting along. Mustn't we, darling?" She transferred her hand to Lazlo's arm.

"'Mustn't'—what a horrid little word," Lazlo said. "But I suppose we should be on our way. It was a pleasure to meet you, Mrs Hart. The best of luck with your hospital."

"But promise me you'll stop with us on your return," said Dolly.

"Yes, of course," said Coral. "I promise."

Coral and Lazlo did not speak until they had returned to the motorway and driven for quite some time. Perhaps because of the distance they had travelled from London—or perhaps because it was later in the day, and so many people's destinations had been achieved—there were far fewer cars on the road, and sometimes, for long stretches, they were the only automobile in sight. The lack of traffic gave Lazlo less opportunity to drive dramatically, and there was something melancholy and wearing about their constant progress.

Coral was just falling asleep when she heard Lazlo speak. "So you did not want to see him?" he asked. She opened her eyes and looked over to see that he had both his hands on the steering wheel. His driving gloves lay crumpled upon the backseat, and his hands looked surprisingly naked and vulnerable without them.

"We didn't have time," said Coral.

"Of course we did," said Lazlo, "if you'd wanted to."

"I suppose I didn't want to, then. It would have been pointless."

"Pointless? What does that mean?"

Coral shrugged. She was looking out the window. The world went by very fast. It was all a blur if you looked straight sideways at it; the only way to see it was to look ahead and to see what was coming. By the time it came, it was gone.

"I don't know. No, I suppose I didn't want to see him."

"Then why did we stop there?"

"It was your idea to stop," she said.

He did not refute this fact, and after a moment he said, "She seemed very jolly."

"Dolly?"

"Yes. Very friendly, she was."

"Yes," said Coral. "She is strange that way."

"You think it is strange to be friendly?"

"Not usually," said Coral. "But yes, in the way that Dolly is friendly. I never understood it."

"You're a dark horse."

"What's a dark horse?" she asked.

"I don't know," he said. "But it's you."

She wanted him to touch her, but both his hands still clutched the steering wheel. She thought that by staring at them she might convey her desire, but she did not succeed. So she reached out and placed her hand upon his leg.

"Don't excite the driver," Lazlo said, but he smiled.


Like so many things that are altered over time, Dolly's philosophy concerning separate bedrooms for married couples was not applied to her second marriage. She looked forward to, and very much enjoyed, the moment when, from opposite sides, she and Clement assumed the great canopied bed that had once belonged to the elderly Mrs Hart. Dolly liked to chatter in the dark. It seemed a good, companionable way to end the day. The idea of drifting into sleep silently frightened her. Talk brightened the darkness; it was a way of reaffirming your existence before succumbing to the void of sleep. Clement was, as always, taciturn, and often fell asleep in the midst of Dolly's monologue, but this in no way bothered her. In fact, she loved the moment when she felt his body slacken and release its burden of consciousness; it was a curious sort of triumph to be awake while he slept, as if he had somehow been humbled or vanquished.

But this night she did not chatter and he did not fall asleep. It was a warm undark night near Midsummer's Eve, and although the bedroom drapes were drawn, there was a sense of the world outside still alive and awake, confused by the unsatisfyingly brief gap between dusk and dawn, in which nothing whole or real could be accomplished.

Clement and Dolly lay in bed tensely awake and rigidly still, in a sort of symbiotic wakefulness. Finally, after what seemed to be several hours of such abeyance, Clement got out of bed. He withdrew himself slowly and quietly, shrugged on his robe and pushed his feet into his slippers, and then stood beside the bed, knowing he could not disappear without remark.

After a moment Dolly said, "Should I not have told you?"

"What?" he said.

"What? About meeting Coral. And her husband. I seriously doubt that they will stop here on their return. They said they would—well, she did—but I know they won't. They seemed so eager to get away."

"Then why did you ask them here?"

"I don't know," said Dolly. "I was so flustered, having her appear out of nowhere like that. I suppose I was only being polite. But no . . . No. I thought you might want to see her, and I knew I should not stand in the way of that."

Clement said nothing. He unloosened and then retied the sash on his dressing gown.

"I suppose I shouldn't have told you," said Dolly.

"Of course you should," said Clement. "Why ever shouldn't have you?"

"Because it has upset you," said Dolly. She reached her hand up into the darkness above her, as if there were something hanging there, just beyond her reach, and then let it drop. She smoothed the coverlet that Clement's withdrawal had disturbed.

"Have I upset you?" she asked.

"No," said Clement. "I'm just going for a walk."

"Outside?"

"Yes," said Clement. "I want some fresh air. Can't sleep."

"Shall I come with?"

"No," said Clement. "Go to sleep."

"I can't," said Dolly. " 'Go to sleep'—such an odd thing to say to somebody, really. It's the one place we can't go to when we're told. The moon as well, I suppose. Even the Amazon jungle or the North Pole I could go to, but not to sleep . . ."

Clement reached across the bed and put his hand on Dolly's cheek, which was damp with tears. He let his gentleness and affection be felt and then removed his hand. "I'm just going out for a little stroll," he said.

Dolly laughed quietly, and said, "Isn't that what God said, before he abandoned us all?"


Clement went downstairs and through the hall into the drawing room. The inside of the house shone with that merciless night-time brightness. They had left the French doors open and he stepped through them, crossed the gravel terrace, and walked out onto the burnt lawn. The summer had been golden and dry so far. Beyond the field of fruit trees, the building equipment stood massively in the nearest of the water meadows, silhouetted darkly against the still glowing sky, the earthmoving tractors holding their trunk-shovels defiantly and frozenly aloft. Clement stared across the field at the blighted landscape. It was inevitable, he knew, this desecration of the earth, and in a way he was glad of it, for it accelerated his detachment from his life: a ruined Hart House would be one less thing holding him close to the world. It was foolish to resist change, for that is all that there was, but nevertheless it did not look modern, it did not look like progress. There was something prehistoric about the spectacle he beheld, as if the world were plunging backwards into darkness.

But not him. He had been rejuvenated. Dolly had seen to it,

sending him to doctors and to a physiotherapist who strapped his legs to a machine that stretched and contorted them and who made Clement kick a medicine ball for hours. And his skin had healed and his muscles had grown limber and strong once again. His stick was stuck among the umbrellas in the copper bucket just inside the front door, a thing of the past. He was able to walk now for as long and as far as he liked, but there was nowhere for him to go.

The Sap Green Forest remained undisturbed. It was to become part of the National Trust, a condition of the transformation of the water meadows into housing estates. The woods would continue to fester in their damp green darkness, holding on to their secret as the world around them was cleared and ruined.

Clement walked across the orchard, through the unremarkable trees, for it was that dormant time of summer when the blossoms have all released their fantastic petals and the fruit has yet to materialise, when the trees are simply trees, and neither beautiful nor bountiful. The footbridge over the stream was in disrepair, but enough boards remained for Clement to cross over, and he followed the path into the woods. It was as warm and still inside the woods as it was outside of them, but the darkness here was more advanced, and a faint dampness lurked in the crevasses and hollows beneath the trees as if this was a hidden enfolded place on the body of the earth.

Clement continued along the path, towards the centre of the woods.

What did it mean, Coral's return to Harrington? Could Dolly have fabricated it, perhaps to test him in some perverse way? He did not think so: he had decided long ago to trust Dolly, and she, as if aware of his trust, was always scrupulously honest with him. She always left well enough alone, and there was little deception or dissembling between them. Perhaps she was wrong; perhaps Coral would appear at Hart House on her return to London. If she did not wish to see him, why ever would she have come to Harrington?

But he reminded himself he had always been wrong about Coral. He remembered the night in London, at Durrants, lying in the empty bathtub, his razor balanced on the rim, within reach, and Coral without. That had been his chance to separate himself from the world, and he had let it pass, because he had hoped. But that was over now.

Dolly loved him, and her devotion somehow prevented the possibility of him relinquishing his life; she had caught him fast to it, for what is love if not wanting someone alive? It seemed incredible to Clement that anyone would value him in this particular way. Coral had not. She had not cared so much whether he was alive or dead, close or far away.

Of course, Robin had loved him, but it had not been a proper love, and he had been right to turn away from it. It had been a thwarted, impossible love, like those blossoms that rot upon the stem and produce stunted fruit, eaten from the inside out by maggots. It was better to have a quiet, decent life than to be a pouf in Brighton.

Near the centre of the woods, where the darkness was most complete, Clement paused for a moment, deep within the copse of holly, which had grown even larger over the years. It was a strange, uncomforting plant, holly, with its crustaceous thorned leaves, defensive and unwelcoming—and from what was it so steadfastly protecting itself? Coral had pushed herself into its heart and encountered the worst sort of violence. She had lost a button in the holly, and other things as well.

The night made some final pivot, bringing morning closer than evening, and exhaled a breath of cool air. A breeze slowly disturbed the trees of the Sap Green Forest. The holly leaves shivered metallically: a strange sound. It was the sound of the world asking once again to be assuaged. Clement turned and began to walk out of the dark woods.